Julia Kavanagh

Seven Years

Vol. 3

Julia Kavanagh

Seven Years
Vol. 3

ISBN/EAN: 9783337342548

Printed in Europe, USA, Canada, Australia, Japan

Cover: Foto ©Andreas Hilbeck / pixelio.de

More available books at **www.hansebooks.com**

TALES.

BY

JULIA KAVANAGH,

AUTHOR OF

" NATHALIE," "ADELE," "THE TWO SICILIES,"

&c. &c.

IN THREE VOLUMES.

VOL. III.

LONDON:

HURST AND BLACKETT, PUBLISHERS,

SUCCESSORS TO HENRY COLBURN,

13, GREAT MARLBOROUGH STREET.

1860.

The right of Translation is reserved.

SEVEN YEARS.

THE TROUBLES OF A QUIET MAN.

CHAPTER I.

It is generally supposed that a quiet temper is conducive of a quiet life. But this is a great mistake, originating in that love of common place which seems inherent to human nature. No man could be quieter than Théophile Durand; few men, according to his own account, and he was strictly veracious, have passed through such tribulation as fell to his lot.

When they began no one knows. He has forgotten it himself, and when they will end it is impossible to divine. Out of this remarkable series we will make a few extracts, showing by what unmerited causes a quiet man became involved in trouble.

Théophile Durand was an employé, and
the employé, or individual employed in any
of the government offices, forms in France,
or rather in Paris, part of a class distinct
in itself, and different from anything of
the same kind here. Every one in Paris
knows the employé, his feelings, habits,
and external signs. There is something
stereotyped and utterly unmistakeable about
the man. Method in matters of feeling, and
sobriety of demeanour, are his two grand
characteristics throughout life.

To this peaceable and timid class belonged
Théophile Durand, the gentlest of gentle
employés. Never did the innocent passion of
caligraphy burn with purer flame than in his
harmless bosom. To transcribe in fair and
legible characters whatever his chef set before
him, was the glory and triumph of Théophile.
Twenty years of his life were devoted to this
important occupation ; from nine in the morning until five in the afternoon he assiduously
bent over the official desk, and longed for no
wider horizon than that of the dull court-yard
of the government office. He was not pro-
moted in rank, nor did he receive any increase
of emolument, but he was not an ambitious

man ; his wants were few, and none ever heard him complain, for in his office as yet trouble had not overtaken him.

This happy existence was at length disturbed by the introduction of a new desk and stool in the quiet bureau, where for years no stranger had appeared. The owner of these portentous signs added to Monsieur Théophile Durand's sense of dismay by his unofficial appearance ; he was a very young man, with something resembling a moustache struggling into existence above his upper lip. He had a thin, sallow, and melancholy, not to say morose-looking, face, and a slender drooping figure. All that Monsieur Théophile could ascertain of him was, that he rejoiced in the name of Auguste Tondu, and entered the office as surnuméraire ; that is to say that he belonged to the class of unpaid employés, condemned to wait for their salary until death or promotion shall make some place vacant in the ranks of their companions.

The desk of the surnuméraire faced that of Théophile, to stare at whom seemed from the very first day his chief task and occupation. He did, indeed, occasionally vary it by sucking and nibbling every pen that came in his way,

or by making little balls of the official paper,
which he entertained himself by masticating,
and, to all appearance, by swallowing ; but
beyond this he did nothing.

The presence of this idle and enigmatical
individual, whom he vainly endeavoured to
draw into occasional discourse, awed and
annoyed Théophile Durand. If ever he looked up from his desk it was to see Auguste
Tondu sucking a pen and looking at him
intently. This happened so often, that at
length Théophile resolved to look up no more;
but this only rendered matters worse, as he
had a ceaseless consciousness that the surnuméraire's eye never left him ; a fact of
which he became firmly convinced, when once
raising his eyes by chance, he met the same
dull and apparently eternal glance fastened on
him still. From that moment Théophile resigned himself to the decrees of fate. He felt
a trouble at hand.

Six months had passed away. Time had
tended to weaken those first unpleasant im-
pressions, and Théophile had grown accustomed to the presence of Auguste Tondu. One
afternoon, as the clock struck five, he rose as
usual from his stool, wiped his pen, put away

his papers, slowly pulled off the black glazed
calico sleeves destined to protect the cloth of
his coat, and was stretching out his hand towards his hat, when a sepulchral voice said:

"Monsieur Durand, will you be good
enough to tell me how long this is to last?"

It was Auguste Tondu, the only employé
besides Monsieur Durand remaining in the
office, who had spoken. Théophile remained
mute. He was in too great a state of surprise
at the unexpected query to think of answering
it.

"Sir," disdainfully resumed the young man,
"I perceive you are dull of apprehension.
My meaning is this. I have been deluded into
the acceptance of this place of surnuméraire
under the impression that you would speedily
die or get promoted; but, sir, you are doing
neither one thing nor the other. I have waited
six months: my patience is exhausted, and I
want to know how long this is going to
last?"

"Sir," rather agitatedly replied Théophile,
"you wish to know more than I can tell. If
my chef is willing to promote me I am quite
willing to be promoted, that is all I can
say."

"And you know nothing about the other thing?"

"No, sir, I do not."

"Upon your word, sir?" continued Auguste, with a suspicious look, that implied he thought Monsieur Théophile better informed on this subject than he chose to confess.

"Upon my word, sir, I know nothing about it; and I may add, sir, that I am not at all inquisitive; I really have no wish to know."

"Well, sir," resumed Auguste, with an oblique look, "you are on your guard; you know that you stand in my way—enough."

Monsieur Théophile uneasily inquired into the exact nature of his meaning, but the only reply he received was the enigmatic "enough," sententiously repeated. He was going to retire in a most anxious foreboding state of mind, when Auguste exclaimed with something like pathos:

"Sir, listen to me, I beseech you. I must unburthen my mind to some one. I have conceived a particular affection for you. Again I say, hear me!"

Why did the tender-hearted Théophile listen to this insidious prayer? but there was the mischief: he must needs be kind and obliging.

Auguste continued :

"You behold in me the victim of circum-stances; a wretched, yes, sir, a thoroughly wretched man."

He did look very desperate as he pursued : "Life is dull, sir, dreadfully dull. I want excitement, genuine excitement. It is a want of my nature ; but I cannot get it, and no one will help me to it. Will you?"

"Sir, be pleased to particularize," gravely replied Théophile, "and I shall see what I can do."

"Sir, you can do nothing; I have been placed here by a perfidious uncle of mine, who declared you were going to die or be pro-moted. Accordingly I find this place narrow. Indeed the whole world is narrow. I have sought, I may say that I have hunted, for the ideal, and never found it. Life is prose, sir, from the beginning to the end of the chapter."

Monsieur Théophile smiled : he began to understand his companion.

"You want excitement," he said, still smil-ing; "get married, my friend, get mar-ried."

Monsieur Tondu seemed to think the

remedy a desperate one indeed, for he growled something or other, and looked suspicious.

" Why did you not marry ? " he asked.

" Because I do not like excitement," was the composed reply.

" Are you sent by my uncle ? " asked Tondu, still suspicious.

Monsieur Durand replied that he had not the honour of knowing Monsieur Tondu's uncle.

" Well, I do not object to marriage by way of change," said Monsieur Tondu ; " indeed I feel that to be loved by a lovely woman would calm me down.   I have a handsome fortune of my own, which my uncle cannot keep from me, and I do not care about a dot.   No, a beautiful, adoring creature, young and accomplished, is all I want."

" How would you like her to be ? " asked Monsieur Durand, " dark or fair ? "

" Fair, fair ! " exclaimed Monsieur Tondu, with a vivacity that scouted the mere idea of raven locks.   " Fair, but by no means red ! "

" Blue eyes ? " suggested Théophile.

" Ah ! heavenly blue ! " ejaculated Auguste, " celestial colour ! "

" A fair complexion ? "

" Lilies and roses ! "

" A sweet temper? "

" A sweet temper! " repeated Auguste, " Monsieur Durand, when shall I see her? "

" Softly, softly," said Monsieur Durand, nodding, " I must speak to her mother first, and to her."

" Tell her I adore her already," enthusiastically exclaimed the young man ; " tell her—"

" Softly, softly, you are not of age. May I know if you are free to marry as you choose? "

" I have ten thousand francs a year, and I shall be twenty-five next month," composedly replied Monsieur Tondu; " only let me see this angel—what is her name? "

" Virginie."

" Only let me see Virginie then, and everything is well."

" You cannot see Virginie before a week," replied Monsieur Durand ; " in the mean while I trust you will be silent."

" As the grave," was the solemn reply, and on that understanding they parted.

" He looks rather young for Virginie," thought Monsieur Durand, as he walked home, " but ten thousand francs a year will make him seem lovely. It is plain, too, that he will

make my cousin happy, but prudence, common prudence, requires that I should make a
few inquiries before we proceed in this
matter."

Monsieur Durand loved plain dealing in all
things. Nothing plainer and more straight-
forward now occurred to him than to step
round to M. Tondu, senior, and sound him
concerning the worldly prospects of his
imaginative nephew.

Monsieur Tondu the elder was a very old
gentleman, who lived in an old house, and
whom Monsieur Durand found sneezing and
coughing by the fire-side. He wore a green
shade to protect his eyes, and sat with his
hands on his knees. From beneath his shade
he peered at Monsieur Durand, and feebly inquired into his errand.

"I am come," began Monsieur Durand,
with a mysterious air.

"Sir," interrupted the old gentleman, with
a cautious forefinger, "sir, take care. I can
stand no emotion, no agitation."

"I trust neither to move nor to agitate
you," replied Monsieur Durand. "I am
come—"

"Does it relate to money?" interrupted the

old gentleman; "I warn you that I neither give nor lend."

"I never ask or borrow," replied Théophile, with great dignity; "please to hear me."

This seemed no easy matter to obtain; for first of all the old gentleman felt sure that there was a draught, then that the chimney smoked, and it was only when Théophile was rising in despair, that the old gentleman said pettishly : "Really, sir, this is very strange. I think you have been here quite long enough to let me know your errand."

"Sir," began Théophile, sitting down, and peering mysteriously into the old gentleman's face, "you have a nephew."

Here a very red-haired lady of some thirty odd years, whom Monsieur Durand had not noticed before, looked from the window where she sat working, and said in rather a masculine voice :

"Well, sir, what if my father has a nephew? are you too come to abuse the poor boy?"

"Oh, her! not a very good character, I fear!" thought Monsieur Durand, "I did well to come." But, though he inwardly congratulated himself on his shrewdness, he declared aloud that he came not to breed family strife, or report evil of the youthful Tondu.

"I only came," he added blandly, "to inquire into a few particulars, such as his age, and the precise epoch when he is to begin and enjoy those ten thousand francs a year."

"Sir, you are very indiscreet," said the red-haired lady, rising as if to leave the room; "my cousin's age and income are no business of yours."

"Sir," said the old gentleman, raising a shaking forefinger, "if that boy has signed bills they are so much waste paper: his debts I will never pay, and he is only a child of nineteen according to law."

"Nineteen!" exclaimed Monsieur Durand, "he told me he was twenty-five, and that he was coming in to ten thousand francs a year next month."

"Outrageous, indelicate!" exclaimed the red-haired lady, who darted angry looks at her father. "You ought not to be answered, sir." But not heeding her, the old gentleman pursued:

"He is nineteen, sir; a lazy, good-fornothing boy, whom I keep out of charity, who has not a sou of his own. If he owes you money, sir, you may bid adieu to it: you will never get it."

"He owes me nothing," impatiently replied Monsieur Durand; "I only want to know when he comes in to those ten thousand francs a year."

"And I insist on knowing your motive for making that extraordinary inquiry," said the lady, with something like majesty.

"Yes," said the old gentleman, "we want to know."

Looking as dignified as either of them Théophile began:

"Monsieur Auguste Tondu, having expressed to me the want of excitement under which he labours, I advised him to marry."

"Very good advice," said the lady.

"He assured me he did not care for money: he only wanted beauty and love."

The lady nodded.

"I accordingly proposed my cousin Virginie Martin."

"Go on, sir," said the lady.

"A beautiful girl, with whom he fell in love on my description."

"Go on."

" For she is fair, not red, and very charming."

" Go on, sir."

" I am going on," said Théophile, a little impatient at this needless spurring, " they are to meet in a week ; to meet will be to love, but Virginie has no money, and I wish to know the truth of Monsieur Tondu's assertion : is he to enter next month on ten thousand francs a year ? "

" Go on," grimly said the lady.

" I will not," indignantly replied Théophile ; " I have said all I had to say."

" Sir, I warned you not to agitate me," exclaimed the old gentleman, and throwing himself back in his chair, he fell into a fit. The lady screamed, and instead of rushing to her father went into violent hysterics.

All presence of mind forsook Monsieur Durand. Instead of assisting his victims, he flew to the door, flew down the staircase, and flew along the street, to the confusion and amazement of all quiet passengers.

We will not describe Monsieur Durand's state of mind. He felt, he knew that he had committed some dreadful mistake, he dreaded meeting the deceitful Tondu, who had led him into all this trouble, and yet meet him he must. Carefully, when that individual entered, did he glance up from his desk, anxiously did he endeavour to read in his face the story of the preceding day's adventure.

Auguste Tondu's face was black as night, but as he gave him, Théophile, no particular share of attention, our friend concluded that, so far as he was concerned, all was right.

He was congratulating himself on his escape, and preparing to depart as four struck, when, with upraised hand, Monsieur Tondu said: "Stop!"

"Stop!" he repeated, "I have something to say to you."

"Tell it to me as we go along," suggested Monsieur Durand, managing to reach the door.

"Right, I shall go home with you," replied Auguste Tondu, taking his arm.

There was no help for it, so Monsieur Durand submitted. As they walked together, Monsieur Tondu said significantly :

"Have you ever had an enemy? No. Well I was scarcely born when my

enemy began. He is my own cousin, much
older than myself, and a monster. We had
not heard of him for a long time, but yesterday he appeared again—but first let me
explain a few matters. I have been reared
by a benevolent uncle, whom I revere, and
I am to marry his daughter, a beautiful
young creature, whom I doat on, and who
has ten thousand francs a year of her own
—you understand?"

"Quite," replied Théophile Durand, "your
cousin is the lady I saw yesterday, and
who—"

"You never saw her," interrupted Monsieur Tondu, with some sternness, "neither
say nor think so. Do not speak: let me
go on. Well, sir, my cousin, after being a
long time invisible, appeared again yesterday. To my revered uncle he painted me
in the most odious colours: as a spendthrift,
in short, as a wretch: to my adored cousin, he
spoke of me as a faithless lover, speculating
on her fortune to marry another woman.
In short, sir, the monster did not leave
the house until my uncle was in a fit and
my cousin in hysterics. On returning home
I found them in that pitiable condition.

Well, sir, what do you think of having an enemy ? "

Monsieur Durand was a quiet man. "Sir," he said dubiously, "how do you know it was your cousin worked all this mischief? "

With the utmost composure Auguste Tondu replied :

"He took an assumed name, something like Bertrand le Grand, but my cousin, who has wonderful perspicacity, recognised him from the first. We have given a description of him to the Commissaire de Police, and he informed us this morning that he is on the track."

"Sir," said Monsieur Durand, with great dignity, "I scorn the falsehood. I will not betray you, but I scorn the falsehood."

A fierce and malignant look was Auguste Tondu's reply. "You wish for war," he said ominously. "Well, then, war you shall have."

Here Théophile's heart failed him. He remembered the manifold opportunities his enemy would possess of annoying him. He already felt pins in his stool, and saw blotches of ink on his fair-written sheets. His proud spirit gave in.

"Well, sir," he said desperately, " I yield,
yes, sir. Your male cousin is a wretch, and
your female cousin an angel."

"Whom you have never seen," suggested
Auguste.

"Never," said Théophile, who soothed his
conscience with the gentle equivocation that
the red-haired lady who said " go on " was not
at all like an angel.

Thus ended this trouble! with peace, it is
true, but with peace bought on such
ignominious terms, that they rankled in
Théophile's mind. He could not endure
the sight of Auguste Tondu; he could not
meet with patience that deceiver's impu-
dent look; in short, he could have no peace
of mind until, on his own request, he was
transferred to another room. Here he
breathed freely and felt happy, until he
made some bitter discoveries, not the least
irritating of which was, that his new stool
was in a constant and refreshing draught.
The other annoyances he had to bear, such
as the employé's conspiring not to let him
see the newspaper, or uniting in an amiable
plot to exclude from him the heat of the stove
in winter, he thought little of: they were

the result of that trouble to which, from the name of its originator, he gave the name of Tondu. "My Tondu trouble" he called it in that private autography which, like every human being, he daily wrote for his own perusal, on the broad sheets of memory.

CHAPTER II.

The second trouble of the quiet man, second on our list, hundredth on his, was even more formidable than that which we have related, and ought to be a warning to all quiet, prudent persons.

Monsieur Durand had a cousin, a widowed lady, named Madame Martin, who had a daughter named Virginie, whom Monsieur Durand was extremely anxious to see fairly married ; perhaps because her mother dropped such strange pertinacious hints, that he could not possibly misunderstand their meaning : she wanted him to marry Virginie. Now though Virginie was amiable, good, and pretty, Monsieur Durand loved celibacy too tenderly to think of relinquishing her company for that of mortal woman, and he hunted out husbands with a praiseworthy pertinacity, that endeared him to the mother, and made him thoroughly odious to the daughter.

His cousin, Madame Martin, a thin and

sharp little woman, resided in one of the quiet
Paris streets, one of those streets where the
houses have shady gardens, full of lilacs and
laburnums ; streets daily becoming more
scarce. Opposite her resided, in one of those
embowered houses, her friend Madame Legrand, a comfortable woman in every sense of
the word, who now and then had a superfluous
floor to let.

Neither in person nor in circumstances were
the two friends alike; but they had one point
of resemblance, they were both " women of
the world." At least they said so, to each
other especially.

If Madame Legrand gave a cosy little dinner
to a quiet little circle of friends, and if instead
of asking Madame Martin and her pretty
daughter Virginie, she asked the two cross,
but rich, old maids opposite, she was the first
to tell her friend of it, with the following
engaging frankness :

" You see, my dear Madame Martin, I would
much sooner have had you and that dear little
Virginie, but what can one do ? those two old
creatures are always loading me with preserves ;
it was only last week they sent me a bottle of
noyau, and another of ratafia ; and then, my

dear Madame Martin, though I do not care one pin about them, yet I am an old woman of the world—that's the truth of it."

Far from being or showing herself offended, Madame Martin admired her friend, and approved her warmly. " Quite right," she replied with emphatic nod and tone, " quite right; that, and no other, was the way to get on through life. She was an old woman of the world herself, and would have done just the same. Invite her and Virginie! why so? What was there to gain by them she should like to know? No, no, ask the donors of preserves, noyau, and ratafia by all means."

Thanks to this philosophic indulgence, the two ladies went on wonderfully well. It is true that occasionally—not more than five or six times a year—Madame Martin would lay various little plots and schemes, rather tending to injure the comforts or interests of Madame Legrand; to deprive her of a good dinner, or prevent her furnished apartment from being let, but even when the said plots and schemes were brought home to her in the most evident manner, she scorned to look disconcerted.

" She was an old woman of the world," she said, triumphantly. This explained everything.

These two excellent friends had, however,
set their heart on a common object: the
marriage of Virginie Martin with some individual, no matter who, rich and high enough
to become the husband of a pretty and charming
girl. That Madame Martin, who had only a
very slender annuity, should wish to get her
daughter advantageously married was natural
enough, but that an old experienced woman of
the world, like Madame Legrand, should trouble
herself about the marriage of any girl, however
charming, might seem strange, but for the
following reasons.

Madame Legrand was something of an
epicure, and she liked a wedding dinner; then
she also liked a handsome present, and every
one knows, or ought to know, that the persons
who help to tie the knot of a French marriage
invariably receive a cadeau proportionate to the
value of the bargain; for a bargain it is in
every sense of the word.

But notwithstanding the zeal of the two
ladies, Virginie remained unmarried. In
vain had the unhappy girl been actually offered
—for it was no less—to every marriageable man
in the vicinity, for the last three years; she
was still Virginie Martin, and yet she was

pretty, and, as we already said, very charming.

Madame Martin was beginning to despair,
and Madame Legrand had prophetically exclaimed that she should never partake of
Virginie's wedding dinner, when the former
lady made an unexpected discovery, which
resuscitated her dying hopes, and filled her
maternal heart with joy.

"Madame Legrand," said she, entering
her friend's little parlour one afternoon, and
addressing the other lady, who was taking
her after-dinner repose near the open
window, "Madame Legrand, we have been
acquainted these twenty years ; we are
both old women of the world, and so what
is the use of finessing with one another?
I might say I called here to see how you
were after your bad cold, but I shall do
no such thing; no, my good Madame Legrand, I called to tell you I am coming
to dine to-morrow with you; Virginie, of
course, accompanies me. What do you
think of that ? " She folded her arms, and
drew herself up with a triumphant air.
Madame Legrand coughed a reserved alarmed

cough, and held herself on the defen-
sive. Her friend smiled and quietly continued :

" I have already ordered a leg of mutton,
and seen about the poultry and the dessert.
But it shall be a very plain meal — extremely so. One must not overdo the thing,
Madame Legrand."

Madame Legrand took an evasive half-
dignified air. She did not exactly understand her friend. She was very dull of
apprehension sometimes. Might she know
exactly what Madame Martin meant? Madame Martin nodded; confessed the request
was reasonable, drew her chair nearer to
that of her friend, took a confidential attitude, and whispered very significantly :

" You see that gentleman walking in
your little garden, do you not ? "

" Yes, I see Monsieur Edouard Lefèvre,
my lodger."

" Then you behold a most unhappy man.
Look at him, is there not grief, yes, deep
grief, written on that face ? "

" Well, he does not look merry ; but what
about it ? "

"Merry! I should like to know how a man who has lost two hundred thousand francs a year could look merry?"

Madame Legrand opened her eyes. Her friend smiled with the consciousness of superior knowledge, and laconically informed her that the simple unassuming man, who had been lodging with her for the last week, was no other than the rich Edouard Lefèvre from Lyons; that unhappy merchant who had recently lost in railroads the heavy sum above mentioned.

"I had it all from my cousin, Théophile Durand," she added, "who had it all from M. Lefèvre's aunt, and who took a fiacre to come and tell me that the unhappy man was here in your house endeavouring to calm his mind."

"But what has all this to do with tomorrow's dinner?" asked Madame Legrand, without losing sight of the original question.

"My dear friend, that unhappy man needs society; it will cheer him."

Madame Legrand looked sceptical. "Well, it really is no use to feign with an old woman of the world like you," said Madame Martin, with philosophic candour, "the fact is, I want him to see Virginie."

"But if he is bankrupt! A propos, I hope he will pay me!"

"Be quite easy," replied Madame Martin, with a sagacious smile, "it is quite true he has lost two hundred thousand francs income — but then he has thirty thousand francs a year left. His aunt said so."

"I would not trust his aunt if I were you," said Madame Legrand, looking uneasy; "indeed, now that I know this I mean to ask him to pay in advance; ay, and this evening too."

Madame Martin was greatly alarmed; it required all her eloquence and tact to persuade her friend that Monsieur Lefèvre had really a handsome fortune left, but she at length succeeded; and, a much easier task, she convinced her that it was highly proper to give him a dinner at her, Madame Martin's, expense, in order to cheer him in his solitude.

"Virginie, do you mean to dress to-day?" dryly said Madame Martin to her daughter on the afternoon of the following day.

The young girl did not answer. She sat near the table, her brow resting on her folded hands ; her whole attitude sad, listless, and drooping.

" Come, make haste," urged her mother, " look at your dress ! how nice it is ! "

The young girl slowly raised her glance. She was a pretty, elegant blonde, with soft blue eyes and delicate features ; but her look was troubled, and her face was pale. She gave a distressed look at the clear white muslin robe her mother displayed with evident complacency, then resumed her old attitude, and wept bitterly. The poor girl knew that dress well, far too well. To her it was the symbol of degradation, mortification, and shame. Whenever a new star dawned on the matrimonial horizon, Virginie Martin had to put on the clear white muslin—nothing became her so well—and display to the best advantage whatever attractions nature had given her. Her whole soul revolted against this, but her mother was inflexible, and poor Virginie was gentle and pretty—she always yielded. On the present occasion she proved more than usually rebellious.

" I cannot and I will not," she passionately

cried, " Heaven help me ! is there nothing I
can do ? let me be a milliner, a dressmaker,
anything you like, but let me earn my bread,
and not do such things." Broken sobs im-
peded her utterance.

" A milliner, a dressmaker ! " exclaimed
Madame Martin, with sorrowful indignation,
" and it is my daughter, Virginie Martin, who
has such ideas, such sentiments ! For shame ! "

" I am not ashamed of them," replied the
young girl, looking up with flushed cheek and
kindling glance, " but I am ashamed whenever
I put on that abominable dress."

" An exquisite white muslin, emblem of
virgin innocence, and youthful freshness, and
transparency of feeling ; she calls it abominable ! "

" Yes, abominable ! for whenever I have put
it on it has been to see myself offered to some
man or other. Good heavens ! the thought of
it makes me feel hot ! When will women
cease to be so cheap ? "

" When they have money," philosophically
replied the old woman of the world ; " I am
really ashamed of your ignorance, Virginie ;
my daughter not to know better ! As to your
being ' offered,' as you choose to call it, I do

not see how it can be helped, whilst men are
what they are.   Entre nous, my dear, men are
regular Turks, and every man thinks himself
a Sultan at the very least.   They like to have
women offered to them, and to pick and
choose.   My dear, let them ; *we* get the best
of it in the end, and, as the old proverb says :
those who laugh last laugh best.   So put on
your dress, and look as pretty as you can."

A fresh burst of tears was the only reply
this maternal exhortation received.

"That is it!" indignantly exclaimed Madame Martin, "cry, redden your eyes, make
yourself look pale, ill, and sulky, as you always do on those occasions ; no wonder the
men will not have so wan and lachrymose a
creature!   Come, do you mean to put on that
dress ?"

Virginie shook her head.   "She could not,"
she said, "she felt she could not."   Madame
Martin was too old a woman of the world not
to know the value of a little pathos now and
then.   She therefore burst into tears, and
lamented her fate in pathetic accents.   "She
had a daughter, and had reared her up for
this !   She had done everything to get her
married, was it her fault if men were not will-

ing? She had carried her maternal devotion to the point of laying out twenty francs—it would not come to less—for a dinner to be given by Madame Legrand, in order that Virginie might meet Monsieur Lefèvre, and now Virginie would not go, and her money was thrown away, and she was a most unhappy mother!"

Virginie resisted a while longer, but at length this matter ended, as usual, by her putting on the white muslin, and agreeing to accompany her mother.

On entering the little parlour of Madame Legrand, Madame Martin was struck with dismay to perceive two ladies, one young, and a very pretty brunette, already seated there. Madame Legrand apologetically whispered that her sister-in-law and niece having unexpectedly called upon her, she could not, of course, do less than ask them to dinner, but then, of course, she would divide the expenses with her friend.

Madame Martin was too old a woman of the world to believe a word of this. The sister-in-law and niece resided ten leagues away, they called twice a year on Madame Legrand; never more; they had evidently been summoned post haste, lest such a prize should go out of the family. It was as clear as noonday. Even for an old woman of the world this was rather hard to bear, and then, to make matters worse, this perfidious Madame Legrand had made the young girls sit side by side. How could the pale inanimate Virginie stand a comparison with the brilliant bloom and engaging vivacity of her rival? Madame Martin internally gave it up, and waited with the resignation of despair for the entrance of Monsieur Lefèvre. But Monsieur Lefèvre did not come. " A sudden fit of indisposition deprived him of the pleasure of dining with the ladies."

Madame Legrand looked disconcerted; her niece pouted; Madame Martin triumphed, and Virginie looked enchanted and charming. Relieved from the dreadful apprehension of meeting the stranger, she became so gay and pretty, that Madame Martin sighed to think how very provoking it was in her never to look so at the proper times. She gave her a good lecture on the subject in the garden, whither they all repaired after dinner. Madame Legrand, her sister-in-law, and niece, held a consultation apart, whilst Madame Mar-

tin and Virginie were unceremoniously left to
their own society.

"Virginie," pathetically said the maman,
"do you wish to break my heart?"

"Is it my fault, maman, if Monsieur Lefèvre
was ill?"

"But if he had come, good gracious, if he
had come! Why, when the door opened
once, you sank back on your seat white and
trembling. For heaven's sake— I hope you
feel better, sir," she suddenly added, in a soft,
insinuating voice.

Virginie looked up, and perceived a serious-
looking man of thirty or so standing near
them. He paused on being thus addressed,
and though not without a keen look of surprise at the elder lady, he politely thanked her,
and said that he felt much better indeed. He
looked inclined to walk on, but Madame Martin was not going to let him escape thus; she
gently compelled Virginie to resume the place
by her side which the young girl had shrink-
ingly left. The path was narrow, Monsieur
Lefèvre could not attempt to move on without
evident rudeness; he did not seek to do so,
but whilst Madame Martin assailed him with
a torrent of fluent speech, he looked at her

daughter with much attention. Evening was
closing in, but they stood face to face within a
few paces of each other: he could see her well.
Virginie was not pale now; she was crimson;
indeed her agitation was so evident, that it was
that, much more than her beauty, which attracted the gentleman's attention. He asked himself with some wonder what there was in his
presence to produce such emotion, and if all
Parisian girls were so. He was not left long
in doubt, for Madame Martin having imprudent-
ly raised her voice, the sound reached the ears
of Madame Legrand, who rushed panting to
the rescue with her blooming, smiling niece.
Monsieur Lefèvre looked annoyed, but he was
now fairly surrounded; there was no help for
it. He submitted with tolerable composure;
walked up and down the garden with the
ladies, and probably begun to understand something of what was going on, for, as he saw
Madame Legrand bring forward her niece on
every occasion, and Madame Martin perti-
naciously offer poor Virginie to his notice, a
scarcely perceptible, though sarcastic, smile
appeared once or twice on his pale firm lips.

"I think we had better go in," at length
kindly said Madame Legrand, who perceived

with some alarm that her guest looked rather
more at the pale Virginie than at her brilliant
niece, "that dear Virginie is so delicate that
the night air might affect her; indeed she
looks very pale as it is!"

Madame Martin indignantly begged to inform her friend that the health of Virginie
was excellent. Virginie had never been ill
since she had the measles.

"Which must have been a good while ago,"
charitably said Madame Legrand.

Madame Martin scorned to answer the
calumny. It refuted itself, or rather Virginie's
youthful face refuted it completely.

They went in; Madame Legrand asked
her niece to sing, and Mademoiselle unhesitat-
ingly attacked a magnificent solo, in which
she introduced a few superfluous ornaments,
that did very well indeed.

"I believe Mademoiselle Martin does not
sing?" kindly said Madame Legrand.

"Yes she does," shortly replied her indignant mother.

Virginie gave her a look of terror. She never
had sung in company in her life, and knew
nothing of music. But her mother was roused
and pitiless. She led her to the piano, and stood

by her side to encourage her, and, if needs were, to enforce obedience. Virginie made an attempt, but her voice broke down almost immediately. " There, you have finished it now," savagely whispered her mother, hurrying her out of the room amidst the ill-repressed titter of the Legrands.

It certainly did not appear that M. Théophile Durand had any particular share in the disasters of this day, save as the originator of the campaign which ended in such signal defeat. But this proved enough, and more than enough, for mother and daughter. Virginie scarcely reached home when she threw herself into a chair, burst into tears, and exclaimed : " I detest Monsieur Durand."

" A mean, spiritless fellow to allow his female relatives to be insulted in that way ! " cried Madame Martin in an excited tone ; " but he shall see, he shall see ! " She resumed her bonnet and shawl, which she had put away, and left the room without any other word.

Monsieur Théophile Durand was in his first nap, when he was roused by a violent ringing and knocking at his room door ; for his apartment consisted of one chamber and a closet. He sat up in bed and listened, slyly feigning deafness. The ringing was violently repeated, and accompanied by something so like the kick of a shoe, that Monsieur Durand wrathfully cried out :

" Who is there ? "

"Open, sir ! " indignantly exclaimed the shrill voice of Madame Martin.

Monsieur Durand chuckled with glee, to think that he had so good an excuse not to admit his cousin.

" My dear relative," he sweetly replied, " I should be charmed, delighted, to let you in, but my night-cap is on. I need say no more to a lady of your quick and delicate perceptions."

" Your night-cap, sir ! how dare you talk of your night-cap to me? What have I to do with it ? "

" Nothing, thank heaven ! " said Monsieur Durand, in a low tone.

" Well, sir," resumed Madame Martin's voice, " I shall go, as you do not choose to let me in. Indeed, I have only this much to say. Having been so ill advised as to act on the information you gave us, my daughter Virginie and I have been drawn in to expense, and have received insults, from which you, sir, will not have the spirit to avenge us. Good night, sir."

Her voice was heard no more, and Monsieur Durand fell in a troubled sleep, from which he awoke three times in a cold perspiration, having dreamed each time that Madame Martin, after forcing her way into his apartment, insisted no longer on his marrying Virginie, but on his marrying *her*, as a slight atonement for the many wrongs he had inflicted on her feelings and her pocket.

Monsieur Théophile would have been calmer in his mind if he had known the unexpected turn affairs had taken.

The feuds of Madame Legrand and Madame Martin never lasted. War is unprofitable, and these two old women of the world knew the value and the blessings of peace.

Madame Legrand quickly found out that her niece would not do, and veered back to Virginie, as a matter of course. Indeed, with such zeal did she enter into the plans she had done her best to frustrate, that she asked Virginie to spend a week with her. The young girl made some resistance, but it was not quite so strong as might have been expected from her previous reluctance to put on the white

muslin. A word of authority from Madame
Martin reduced her to obedience.

For two days Madame Martin, who was supposed to be in the country, kept herself locked
up. Early on the morning of the third day
she slipped over to Madame Legrand's, and
was admitted to a mysterious interview in that
lady's bedroom.

"And how are matters going on?" asked
Madame Martin.

"Well, well," calmly replied Madame Legrand. "Monsieur Lefèvre is enamoured, I
saw that from the first."

"And how does Virginie behave?" asked
Madame Martin, "like a fool?"

"Not exactly. She does not give Monsieur
Lefèvre many opportunities of meeting her;
but I rather fancy that her timidity and
bashfulness are advantageous. He already
lends her books."

"That's good," approvingly said Madame
Martin.

"Excellent. And now, my dear friend,
if it is to be a match, I may as well tell you
what I should like. I am moderate by nature.
A dozen of silver forks and spoons will do."

"My dear Madame Legrand," replied Madame Martin, with a placid nod, "nothing can repay a friendship like yours. If Virginie becomes Madame Lefèvre, she owes it to you."

"Perhaps your cousin might think," began Madame Legrand.

"*He!*" interrupted Madame Martin, with great scorn, "I should like to see *him* expecting anything. The mean little fellow."

With this eulogy Madame Martin went back to her apartment, but lest her dear friend Madame Legrand should take a real fancy to send back Virginie, she, Madame Martin, thought it her wisest course to go off to Neuilly on a visit to an aged aunt, who was too far gone in age to protest against the intrusion. What could she say, moreover, when her niece entered the house with the avowed intention of making her comfortable?

"I do not see, aunt, why I should not stay with you, now that Virginie is going to get married," she said graciously.

"Is she going to get married?" asked the aunt, lifting up a feeble head, "and with whom?"

"With Monsieur Lefèvre of Lyons," replied Madame Martin.

" Not the one who has two wives already,"
said her aunt, musingly.

" Two wives !" echoed Madame Martin, in a
hollow voice.

" Yes, he was married abroad, and he married another lady in France, and there was a
great law-suit about which was the right
wife."

" It cannot be that one," said Madame
Martin ; " I will never believe," she added,
raising her voice, as if the culprit were within
hearing, " I will never believe that, bad as he
is, my cousin Théodore Durand could help to
delude Virginie into such a marriage as that."

The aunt burst into a croaking laugh.

" Oh !" she cried, lifting up her hands, " if *he*
had anything to do with it I consider it a
settled thing. Poor Virginie, poor girl."

It was night, but Madame Martin's resolve
was taken in a second. She sent for a cab,
jumped into it, and drove to her cousin's door,
for wrath proved stronger, in this instance, than
maternal anxiety.

Unconscious of the brooding storm, Monsieur Théophile Durand, who was an economical man, was cooking his dinner on a stove in
the closet, when a mild, deceitful ring at the

door induced him to open it. In bounced
Madame Martin, wrathful and smiling.

"Good afternoon, sir," she said sweetly, "I
hope you are well, sir?"

"Quite well," faintly replied Monsieur
Durand. "Pray be seated."

"Thank you, sir, a carriage is waiting for
me at the door. Perhaps you will kindly
answer me this question, sir, How many wives,
to your knowledge, has Monsieur Lefèvre got?"

"Tw—o," gasped Monsieur Durand, "but
the second is the right one. I learned it yesterday."

"Thank you, sir, I am very much obliged to
you. I have it from your own lips, on your
confession that you advised me to marry my
daughter to a man that has two wives living."

"My dear cousin, I thought him single."

"Did you inquire?" was the stern rejoinder.

"No—o."

"Then how dare you speak of Monsieur
Lefèvre to me, sir?"

"But you know all about it!" desperately
exclaimed Monsieur Durand.

"I sir, I! Do you mean to add insult to
injury?"

"But when you came the other evening

and rang, when I had my night-cap on, you knew it surely!"

Madame Martin loftily begged he would neither recall that evening nor his conduct thereon, and again asked if he meant to add insult to injury.

Monsieur Durand, who was losing his temper, testily replied that he meant to eat his dinner, and unceremoniously returned to the closet and to his cooking.

"Very well, sir," resumed the voice of Madame Martin from the outer room, "very well, sir, you will remember this."

The slam of a door told Monsieur Durand that she was gone. His first selfish, natural feeling was one of self-congratulation at escaping her tongue, and being allowed to eat his hard-earned dinner in peace. Then came remorse and concern at the error into which he had fallen, and an earnest desire to mend matters, so far as they could still be mended.

Monsieur Théophile Durand had a good deal of that nervous timidity which lies most in manner, and does not exclude courage. His bravery, for lying dormant, was none the less real; he now got excited about the wrongs of Virginie, and resolved to right them without loss of time.

"The cold-hearted villain!" he exclaimed, seizing his hat and cane, and hurrying out, " did he think that poor child had no protector, no friend? We shall see—we shall see."

Monsieur Durand lived at no great distance from Madame Legrand's house. In a few minutes he had reached her door, and was knocking violently. A frightened-looking servant answered the call.

" Madame is out," she said.

" I want to see Monsieur Lefèvre," sternly replied Théophile; "lead me into his presence."

The servant afterwards declared he looked quite awful, and that resistance was out of the question. Without even asking his name, she opened a door and ushered him into the room where Monsieur Lefèvre was sitting with Virginie.

This requires explanation. Monsieur Lefèvre, as Madame Legrand plainly saw, was very much smitten with her young friend, and readily availed himself of every opportunity of meeting her, which the elder lady afforded him. From lending books, he soon came to giving Virginie music lessons; Madame Legrand was present, of course, but the lessons were long, and she sometimes left the room, to return almost immediately, it is true. But this day Madame Legrand left and did not return; she forgot Virginie, propriety, and prudence. Her cook had allowed her apricot preserves to burn; an unmistakable odour reached her in the drawing-room. She rose precipitately, rushed down-stairs, and found the jam on the fire and the kitchen deserted. The faithless cook was flirting with the butcher's boy at the garden gate, " and my apricots, my most valuable apricots," as Madame Legrand afterwards said in relating this lamentable occurrence to a friend, " were left to their fate."

Desperate emergencies inspire desperate resolves. Madame Legrand took up the hissing jam, called the cook, gave her warning on the spot, then solemnly bade the housemaid deny her to the whole world.

" Give me a white apron," she said, " and no matter who comes, say I am not at home."

Thus Virginie remained alone with Monsieur Lefèvre. Neither the teacher nor the pupil were at first conscious of this important fact. Monsieur Lefèvre, happening to turn his head round, first perceived that Madame Legrand was gone. Virginie next, appealing to that lady, became aware of her absence, and of what was infinitely worse in decorous France, that she, Virginie Martin, was alone with her music-master. What should she do? To leave precipitately might look like an affectation of prudery, to remain might make Monsieur Lefèvre hold her forward or imprudent. Still something must be done. She hesitated a while, then at length, and with a painful blush that betrayed her embarrassment, she rose, and closing the piano, said as calmly as she could:

"I have troubled you enough to-day: Madame Legrand may want me below, I shall go and see."

Monsieur Lefèvre looked undecided; but by the time Virginie had crossed the room and reached the door, his mind was made up, and following her quickly, he arrested her with the entreaty:

" May I request that you will hear me
for a few moments?" Virginie remained with
her hand on the lock, and by her silence
gave consent.

What passed, and what Monsieur Lefèvre
said, need not be told. Of course it was a
declaration of love and an offer of marriage.
Virginie's reply we need not record, of course
it was modest assent.

Love is a beautiful thing; but for a man
to declare his affection to a woman is by
no means so delightful a task as might be
imagined, and for a woman to hear the
aforesaid declaration, even when it comes
from a preferred lover, is not always so
pleasant as might seem. It is often quite
a relief when a third unconscious person
steps in and breaks on the awkward, how-
soever rapturous, silence that must needs
follow.

On the general principle, therefore, Théophile Durand ought to have been welcome
to both Virginie and her lover; but strange
to say, whether his interruption came a
little too soon, that is to say, before the
rapture had subsided and the awkwardness
had come, or a little too late, that is, after

the said awkwardness was quite over and his presence no longer needed,—somehow or other, in short, he came most unseasonably, startling by the abruptness of his entrance the fair Virginie, who was sitting on a sofa, and who, on seeing him, got up with a little scream, and considerably annoying her companion, who rose more slowly from the couch, and returned with interest the scowl of Monsieur Théophile Durand.

"Sir," he sharply said, "who are you? What do you want?"

"Virginie, take my arm and leave this house," was Monsieur Durand's indignant reply.

On hearing an utter stranger call his mistress by her Christian name, Monsieur Lefèvre reddened and looked angry. Whilst Virginie made a motion of disgust, and said sharply:

"I beg, Monsieur Durand, that you will not meddle in my concerns."

"Infatuated girl!" said Monsieur Durand, filled with pity for her blindness, "do you know this man? Child, he has two wives living! Two wives."

Monsieur Lefèvre laughed scornfully.

" The accusation is too ridiculous for me to resent it," he said, calmly, " and I am sure Mademoiselle Martin will not credit it one moment."

" Not one," said Virginie, with great warmth, " not one."

" I repeat it, he has two wives," said Monsieur Durand, warming with his subject, " a poor young Indian girl, whom he married in the South Sea Isles, and a lady of Lyons—"

" Sir, I will hear no more on this absurd matter," interrupted Monsieur Lefèvre, waxing wroth.

" Virginie, take my arm and leave the house," said Monsieur Durand; " I tell you this man has two wives, that your mother is distracted with grief on your account, and that she insists on your leaving this wretched house."

Monsieur Lefèvre looked stiff and offended.

" If Madame Martin had done me the honour of requesting a personal explanation," he said, " all this would have been avoided. I know, of course, that she will regret her precipitate conduct, but I do not know how far I can consent to overlook such unmerited insults."

And without giving Virginie a look, Monsieur Lefèvre left the room. The young girl burst into tears; but Monsieur Durand took her arm and led her away, asking indignantly if she regretted not marrying a man who had two wives living.

It was lucky Madame Martin lived opposite; Virginie could scarcely cross the street, and Monsieur Durand thought she would surely faint on the staircase. He was the more frightened that Madame Martin was out. The portress had given the key of their apartment to Virginie as they passed her lodge; for this strange mother, instead of snatching her child from the fangs of the bigamist, had left word that she was gone back to Neuilly.

" There is something dreadful under all this," thought Monsieur Durand, foreseeing a calamity; "I must lock up Virginie, take a cab and rush off to Neuilly, there I shall warn Madame Martin that I have rid her of this determined bigamist, then, *ma foi*, I shall wash my hands of the whole affair." So said, so done. Virginie, though weak and

faint, declared she could remain alone, and
Monsieur Durand took care to lock her up slyly,
and walk off with the key in his pocket.
A cab was soon found, and in less than an
hour Monsieur Durand entered the house of
Madame Martin's aunt.

The two ladies were at dinner when he
was announced.

"Monsieur Durand!" said Madame Martin,
laying down her fork, "what has he been
doing?"

"Show him in—show him in," said the
old aunt, with feeble eagerness, "I know it
will be something funny."

In walked Monsieur Durand, cool, dignified,
and important. "Madame," said he to the
aunt, "I must apologize"—

"Never mind, never mind," she interrupted, "what is it?—let us hear it."

"Cousin," said Théophile, addressing Madame Martin, "Virginie is safe."

Virginie's mother heard him with singular
calmness.

"What about it?" she asked.

"I locked her up myself in your home,"
pursued Théophile, "and here is the key of
your apartment."

Madame Martin stared, but did not utter one word.

"I may say that I have saved her," pursued Monsieur Durand. "I found her alone with that wretch, and from her gently-confused look I have no doubt he had been making love to her. But I exposed him to her, cousin; exasperated him so that he pretty clearly gave her up, and left the room in a great pretence of anger; upon which I took her arm, forcibly led her out, locked her up, and came here."

Monsieur Durand wiped his forehead, and smiled complacently on his cousin.

"I knew it!" cried Madame Martin, striking her plate with her knife, and thus recklessly breaking it in the exasperation of her anger; "I knew it—he has ruined all —all ruined—ruined." Monsieur Durand heard her amazed.

"Miserable man," she resumed, "what made you meddle? just tell me that; could you not let a mother judge for her child?"

"A bigamist!" began Monsieur Durand.

"A bigamist!" screamed Madame Martin, "he a bigamist, a distinguished Professor of Eloquence in the University of Louvain, at

a salary of six thousand francs a year, if
not ten,—he a bigamist? Say that you are a
bigamist, sir!"

"I?"

"Yes, sir, a bigamist, I maintain it."

Here a gurgling noise was heard, and it
was discovered that the old aunt was choking
in her arm-chair, the result of indiscreet
laughter.

"Wretch!" said Madame Martin, flying
to her aid, "did you come here to commit
murder?"

She slapped her aunt in the back, until the
venerable lady came round, and though still
much exhausted, partly recovered her breath.
This satisfactory result being obtained,
Madame Martin declared that, thanks to her
obliging cousin Monsieur Durand, she must
have another jaunt to Paris, and, without
finishing her dinner, she threw on, rather than
she put, her bonnet and shawl, and accompanied by the discomfitted Durand, she walked
down to the cab, informing the cabman that
if he drove quick his fare would be doubled.

Madame Martin was too much exasperated
to scold her unfortunate cousin. She merely
asked, with keen and cutting irony, how a man

of his bright wit and experience could take a refined professor of eloquence for a coarse merchant and a bigamist, and how he dare take on himself to lock up Virginie? and as Monsieur Durand was too much cast down to reply, she maintained a sulky silence until the cab stopped at her door. She then alighted, and sternly said:

"Here we part, sir. Your conduct I will not qualify. You have covered yourself and your family with disgrace, you have done your best to prevent my daughter Virginie from making a most excellent and desirable match. Your work is consummated. Go; I request that I may never see your face again."

So saying, Madame Martin majestically entered the house, slammed the door in her cousin's face, and left him the cab to pay.

"Two francs for going, one franc for waiting, and four francs for having driven fast back to Paris: seven francs, besides what Monsieur chooses to give," added the cabman.

"Take it, take it all!" desperately cried Monsieur Durand, throwing him the money and running away.

CHAPTER III.

THAT Virginie was married, that the wedding dinner was choice, that the bride looked
lovely, and the bridegroom thoroughly blessed,
Théophile Durand learned through report.
But he was not asked to the marriage ceremony, he was not one of the dinner guests;
"and though without me the two ungrateful
creatures would never have been married,"
said Monsieur Théophile Durand, " I received
my usual reward : neglect."

Under this mortifying neglect Monsieur
Durand was not doomed to linger.   His new
cousin ended by laughing at the bigamist
story; Virginie was too happy to feel any re-
sentment, and Madame Martin magnanimously
declared that she forgave her cousin : in short,
the three united in extending the hand of peace
to the offender.   Monsieur Théophile Durand
was formally asked to dinner : being a good-
natured man, and having at heart a foolish

liking for his kindred, he accepted the invitation. The dinner was strictly a family dinner, but in honour of the reconciliation, a little soirée followed it.

"And now," thought Théophile Durand, "my troubles in this quarter are surely over. Virginie is married. I have made ample apologies to her husband, who is a very agreeable fellow when he is not excited, and Madame Martin does not appear to entertain the least matrimonial design upon me. Yes, I think I am really safe in that quarter." So thought and soliloquized the deluded man, never suspecting the world of trouble that awaited him.

We have seen that the reconciliation dinner to which Théophile Durand had been asked was followed by an evening réunion, quite select. Madame Martin whispered to her cousin : " I could not ask Madame Legrand nor *that* set. No, my son-in-law's position would not allow it."

The réunion was more than select ; it was decidedly thin, and its successor—for Madame Martin insisted that Virginie should receive every Thursday evening—was too select for Monsieur Lefèvre's taste. From nine o'clock

Madame Martin and her daughter sat in the
gaily-lit drawing-room, vainly waiting for
visitors, who came not. At ten, indeed, Théophile Durand made his appearance in correct
evening costume, but, to the vexation of Virginie, and to her husband's evident annoyance,
not a soul besides.

As eleven struck Monsieur Lefèvre said to
his wife:

"Another such evening, my dear, and we
will give up parties."

"It is very annoying," said Virginie, "I had
provided refreshments and cakes,—and now
they are wasted, as it were. We do not want
them."

"It is tiresome," said Madame Martin, "but
we must try again."

Monsieur Lefèvre did not answer. It was
plain that only politeness prevented him from
giving a flat denial.

Madame Martin was annoyed at the evening's failure, and alarmed for the future. Her
son-in-law was kind and courteous, but he was
not manageable. He had already shown a
strong inclination to authority, not despotism
certainly, but authority under any aspect was
distasteful to Madame Martin; it did not let

her have her own way, which she was naturally
fond of. Like a prudent woman as she was,
she avoided struggles: Monsieur Lefèvre
would not be controlled or managed, but he
might be led gently. To lead him skilfully
was therefore her object: but how was she to
do so in this present matter?

"What can I do if the people will not
come?" she said confidentially to Théophile
Durand, "we asked twenty, and you see not
one came."

" Ask forty," shrewdly said her cousin.

"Forty!" exclaimed Madame Martin, with
a start, "and where should we put them?
Our drawing-room is so small."

"They will not come," replied Monsieur
Durand. "The twenty did not come; the
forty will no more come than the twenty; but
forty people will have had the compliment paid
them of being asked, and you will not have
had the trouble of receiving them."

This was an idea; Madame Martin felt it
was a valuable one too; but, casting an
alarmed look towards her son-in-law, she
whispered to Théophile Durand: "Speak low,
I entreat you. Edouard is so peculiar, so
matter-of-fact, so literal, that he would never

ask more people than he wished to see; but I
shall certainly follow the plan you suggest;
how to do so I do not yet know; but where
there is a will there is a way."

A way Madame Martin certainly found.
She asked not forty, but fifty people, and
chose them so judiciously, that when her son-
in-law expressed his surprise at seeing persons
drop in whom he had not asked, and she carelessly replied: "I just asked them to fill up
in case the others should not come," he expressed his satisfaction at her prudence.

From this it will be readily gathered that
the third party was more successful than the
two first. Fortune favoured, indeed, Théophile
Durand's suggestion: fifteen people mustered;
ten belonged to the original twenty, and five
to the additional number asked by Madame
Martin. She expressed her satisfaction to
Théophile Durand, by asking him once for
all.

"Yes, cousin," she said suavely, "you
are always welcome. Virginie and her husband have quite a regard for you, and I trust
you know and feel the esteem in which I hold
you. Our last evening flagged a little; my
floating debt, as I call my superfluous invités,

did not come in well. We had a dearth of black coats. Suppose you send us a sprinkling of your friends the employés."

"With great pleasure," replied Théophile Durand, who delighted to oblige, and in his generosity he forgot the soreness he had felt on seeing Madame Martin plume herself on the success she owed to his advice, but which she did not dream of acknowledging to her son-in-law.

He set to work that same day ; he spoke to his chef, Monsieur Randon, a lofty man not easily propitiated, but with whom he was a bit of a favourite. He had the good fortune to find the potentate in an excellent temper.

"I see, I see," he said, "a young couple who require encouragement ; well, Durand, I like to encourage such. I shall go ; Madame Randon shall go. What is there to be?"

"Music, I believe, and a young poet is to repeat some verses."

"I like poetry," said Monsieur Randon, "and a game of cards."

"My cousin is a first-rate écarté player," eagerly said Théophile.

"I like cards and refreshments," continued Monsieur Randon.

" Virginie is profuse with refreshments, platefuls of cakes, ices, &c."

" I shall go," paternally said Monsieur Randon, " I like to encourage struggling merit. Tell your cousins, Durand, that they may rely upon me and Madame Randon."

Théophile Durand delivered the message to Madame Martin, who on hearing the tidings threw her arms around his neck, and called him an angel.

Everything promised well, yet one of those mysterious presentiments which, in our ignorance, we do not sufficiently regard, warned Théophile Durand to stay at home, and go to bed on that fatal Thursday. Kindness prompted him to do the very reverse. " My poor cousin wants me," he thought, " her floating debt, as she calls it, runs short. My presence is necessary. True, I should like home and quiet best ; but we must not be selfish." Supported by these generous and philanthropic feelings, Monsieur Durand dressed himself and walked off to Monsieur Lefèvre's house.

Carriages encumbered the door.

" Oh, ho ! " thought Monsieur Durand, " some one else has a party in my cousin's house. Well, truly, why not ? " And not altogether displeased to show a stylish group of ladies in ample muslin, and gentlemen in white cravats, who were coming up the staircase behind him, that he too was going to a party, Théophile Durand gave a sharp, jerking ring at his cousin's door. But the ladies stopped behind him. Were they, too, invited to Madame Lefèvre's evening party? They were, there could be no doubt about it.

The door opened, and a fragrance of smoke issued forth.

"Is the place on fire?" asked Monsieur Durand, stepping back.

"No, sir," replied the servant, "but we have been obliged to make fires in all the rooms, and some of the fires will not burn."

"Dreadful," said one of the ladies, "I hate smoke."

The servant-girl looked at the speaker and her companions, then asked in a peculiar tone:

"Are you ladies coming to us? Perhaps it is up-stairs you are going?"

"Madame Lefèvre," replied one of the gentlemen.

"Walk in," said the servant, "but you'll get no room, that's all."

" No room ! " they all exclaimed in a breath.

" There has been no room since half-past nine," replied the servant; " the drawing-room has been full since eight: the two bed-rooms are full ; the dining-room is full, and the ante-room is crammed."

They stared incredulous and amazed, but they soon acquired melancholy confirmation that the servant had spoken truly. As she closed the door upon them, they found themselves in a smoky ante-room, hemmed in on every side by people all standing, and none of them in the best of tempers. The new-comers were stared at in rather an ungracious fashion, and a lady in blue, who had a sharp nose, said with great asperity of tone and manner:

" There is decidedly an hour beyond which people ought not to come to parties : it is ridi-culous. May I ask what you are treading on my dress for, sir?" she added, looking dag-gers at Théophile Durand.

He apologized with the greatest humility, but excused himself on the plea of a desire to get into the drawing-room. The lady with the sharp nose giggled hysterically.

" And do you suppose, sir," she asked,

" that we, who have been standing here this
hour without being able to get in, are going
to let you in ? No, sir, you came last, and out
you shall stay."

The ladies in muslin, who had entered with
Théophile Durand, looked lofty and mildly
disgusted.

" Oh ! people may look at me," said the
lady with the sharp nose. " I do not care ;
but those who came last shall not get in first.
It is bad enough to stand two hours and not
to be offered a biscuit or a glass of water."

Here a stir took place in one of the inner
rooms, and a male voice was heard entreating :

" Pray let us out. Let me beg for a little
room. We only want to get out."

" It is very extraordinary," said the lady
with the sharp nose, " that after being in such
a hurry to get in and prevent other people
from enjoying what there is to be enjoyed,
some people will insist on disturbing others
and getting out again. I think for my part
they should be kept in."

But the rumour that a lady was fainting
opened a passage to a stout gentleman, who
appeared half bearing, half dragging, an
equally stout lady. In vain the lady with the

sharp nose protested that this was but a mean and shallow artifice to deprive last comers of their rightful places, and that it should be resisted. The red face of the stout gentleman was bathed in genuine perspiration, and there was no mistaking the zeal with which he bore and dragged the stout lady after him.

" A chair, for Heaven's sake," he gasped, as he got out of the crowd ; " is there no one that will have the charity to get me a chair ? "

" Chairs ! " giggled the lady in blue, " does Monsieur suppose that if there were chairs ladies would remain standing for two hours ? "

Monsieur was going to declare desperately that he supposed nothing, when his eye caught that of Théophile Durand, who was vainly hiding in the crowd, and who turned pale on meeting it : the stout gentleman was his chef, his superior.

" Oh ! you are here," said Monsieur Randon, with smooth sarcasm, " may I request you to help me to support Madame Randon ? "

Théophile obeyed, and assisted in propping Madame Randon, who was slowly recovering, and whom her husband soon entirely surrendered to his employé's care. Being thus relieved from a considerable burden,

Monsieur Randon wiped his damp forehead, and, regardless of place or time, thus addressed his subordinate :

" Well, sir, I congratulate you. So this is the little intellectual soirée you asked me to patronize, and to which like a deluded man I brought a dozen of friends and their innocent families ! Sir, you are an impostor," added Monsieur Randon in his wrath. " Come, my love," he added, taking the arm of his wife, who gave Théophile a withering glance for his pains, " let us leave this ill-fated house, where people are smothered, smoked—and starved," added Monsieur Randon, with bitter emphasis.

They stalked out; Théophile Durand remained stunned, heedless of the sarcastic looks the lady in blue cast upon him. Then, suddenly awakening to the fearful consequences this untoward event might produce on his prospects, he rushed down-stairs, hoping to overtake Monsieur Randon, to mollify his wrath by humble apologies. But Monsieur and Madame Randon had entered their carriage, and were already rolling away.

Théophile Durand was roused. Was this the reward he got for endeavouring to serve his cousin? Randon, the great Randon, had been alienated for ever, and for what? for want of due politeness and attention, for want of an ice or a plateful of cakes.

"She shall hear a piece of my mind!" desperately exclaimed Monsieur Durand, and remembering that it was useless to go up the front staircase, he went up by the back or kitchen staircase, undignified but sure. No sooner had he tapped at the kitchen door than it flew open. On the threshold within appeared Madame Martin pale and breathless.

"Where are the ices?" she exclaimed, "speak, sir, where are they? Have you brought the cakes at least? No; then pray, sir, what are you a limonadier for?"

"I am not a limonadier," said Théophile, "I am your injured cousin."

"My dear creature," cried Madame Martin, clasping both his hands, "run for ices, run for cakes, run for anything. Where the people are come from I do not know; but they keep pouring in. The place is full, three ladies have fainted already. Go, now do, there is a good soul. There is a pastry-cook round the corner, who sells odds and ends at two francs a

pound, and procures ices as cheap. Here
is money, go, pray go."

She shut the door in his face, and Monsieur Durand found himself with silver in
his hand on a black landing.

He was a good-natured man: he forgot
his wrongs in his cousin's calamities. He
went for the ices; he went for the cakes.
He went not once, but three times. By
twelve his labours were over, the people
had discovered that there was nothing
more to be had by staying, and they departed slowly. By this time, too, Monsieur
Durand's wrath had cooled, and he magnanimously resolved not to crush his cousin
with the name of Randon. "The poor
thing has had trouble enough," he gener-
ously thought, "let her rest; let her rest."

But generosity is a delusion; with a
sigh of relief Monsieur Durand was preparing to depart, when Madame Martin
solemnly begged him to enter her son-in-
law's study: there Théophile found his
cousin black as night.

"Sir," he said, "I can scarcely credit,
and I certainly cannot qualify, the extraordinary statement I have just received from

Madame Martin, that for the painful and disgraceful scenes which took place here this evening I am indebted to you; that you took the liberty of inviting to this house something like thirty or forty of your personal friends, making me and my domestic arrangements a matter of ridicule and amusement to them. I repeat, sir, comments are superfluous: but I beg to assure you, that this second breach will not be so easily repaired as the first."

Monsieur Lefèvre rose, bowed stiffly, and left the room.

Théophile Durand remained dumb. He had incurred the wrath of Monsieur Randon, he had been made an errand boy of, and now he was snubbed. The cup was full. He went home, took to his bed, and was ill a week.

This is the last trouble on record of a quiet man; that it will be the last no one who has perused the preceding pages will readily believe.

YOUNG FRANCE.

TANCREDI P. MATHIEU was a member of the Young France party, when there was a Young France, which is now some years ago. He was the son of an honest and wealthy Parisian grocer, who allowed him a handsome income and total liberty of action.

Our hero's real name was Pierre Mathieu. Tancredi had been assumed for poetical and euphonious reasons. His friends, who knew his sensitiveness on that head, never gave him any other appellation. Like the whole Young France brotherhood, Tancredi wore long curly hair, a narrow pointed hat, white kid gloves, and a shirt collar turned down with the most Byronian despair. Any one who looked on that shirt collar could have told that its owner was a melancholy man—one " whose young aspirations had been nipped in the bud by the chilling breath of an unfeeling world."

Tancredi's existence had indeed been embittered by several severe disappointments. In the first place, he was neither an un-known foundling, nor an exile, nor a persecuted man : he had enjoyed throughout life the most provoking and commonplace happiness. He did not possess the comfort of having a tyrannical father. Monsieur Mathieu the elder was the soul of good nature. Easy, placable, and fond of peace, he allowed Tancredi to have his way. There is no denying he would have liked to see his son at the head of a thriving business, but since his vocation did not lie in that direction he raised no opposition to his joining the Young France tribe, wearing long hair and a pointed hat. Some persons kindly assured him that Pierre—they scorned to call him Tancredi—was on the high road to ruin. But Monsieur Mathieu composedly replied that his son was only afflicted with a temporary mania, then very prevalent amongst young Frenchmen, and that he did not despair to see him one, day radically cured. This conviction did not prevent the grocer from reasoning with his son ; he even endeavoured to show him

that he was acting very foolishly; but as
Tancredi immediately assumed the tone and
attitude of a martyr, and as his father—
who, under the appearance of great sim-
plicity, was, nevertheless, possessed of much
shrewdness and good sense—perceived that
he longed to be persecuted for his opinions,
he gradually dropped the subject, and left
him thoroughly free.

Tancredi keenly felt what he termed his
father's injustice. He was at war with
society—so at least he said—and he had a
right to persecution. His friends all agreed
with him that it was a hard case, but advised him, however, to bear with it patiently.
His bosom friend, Charlemagne Champion
by name, for imperial and chivalrous ap-
pellations were rife in their circle, comforted him as best he might.

" My good fellow," he said, with an odd
twinkle in his eye, " fathers will be so—
provoking—perverse—doing the very things
they should not ; but better times are
coming."

And Charlemagne Champion, who, though
Young France, was suspected to have some

of the Old France wag in him still, squeezed
his friend's hand with expressive warmth.

But Monsieur Mathieu's irritating pass-
iveness was not Tancredi's only cause of
grief: another source of bitter regret lay in
his personal appearance. Somehow or other
he had inherited from his father the grocer,
a round, rosy, good-humoured face, of which
he could not possible get rid. Notwithstanding his constant efforts to infuse into it
some slight portion of the poetical melancholy which, to use his own words, " was
devouring his soul," it always looked pleased,
happy, and contented. To make matters
worse, he was remarkably fair, and inclined
to corpulency. Gladly would Tancredi
have sacrificed half his worldly hopes to be
thin and sallow. Accordingly, when Charlemagne Champion spoke of better times, he
sighed, shook his head, and casting a de-
spondent look at the glass, he asked in a
hollow voice, " Charlemagne, will that face
ever change? "

" I hope not," composedly replied
Charlemagne, " it is the living likeness of
the immortal Robespierre." Tancredi gave a
start.

" Like him—I am like him ! " he exclaimed.

" Do you not see it ?"

" Why, yes," musingly replied Tancredi, "you are quite right, I do see something in the contour. Robespierre was a minister, but I am not sorry to be like him."

Thus comforted, Tancredi took heart. Besides, like all generous spirits, our hero often forgot his own unhappiness in his philanthropic compassion for the ignorance and blindness of mankind at large; he was convinced that the world was not yet half civilized, and that the bourgeois of Paris, especially, were in a lamentable state of barbarism. As he was himself a bourgeois by birth, he conceived that his " mission " must plainly lie in civilizing his unhappy brethren, and as he happened to entertain for them the most thorough and hearty contempt, he was evidently peculiarly fitted for this delicate task.

The bourgeois are the middle classes of France. They chiefly consist of retired tradespeople, small capitalists, and employés, or clerks, in the offices of the government, from whom they generally receive a moderate salary for their services. They are a quiet

and inoffensive race, but remarkably timid and
cautious, and tenacious of their habits and
opinions to an extraordinary degree. Seeing
them so far behind their age, Tancredi gener-
ously resolved to devote himself to their
improvement. Whether they were willing to
be improved or not was no consideration;
indeed Tancredi did not care a pin on the
subject. If he could not succeed in making
the bourgeois better, he had little doubt of
getting persecuted by them; so that, which-
ever way the wind blew, he felt pretty sure
of reaping some benefit. These preliminaries
being settled, he resolved to begin his attack
on a little colony of bourgeois, which had
been settling for the last century in one of
the most quiet and retired streets of the
Marais, not far from the spot where stood his
father's house.

This street, which shall be nameless, very
much resembled a country town. Though
not possessing more than a dozen houses on
either side, it was divided into several sets,
which knew nothing whatever of one another. The most important set, and that
which immediately drew Tancredi's attention,
was Madame Jacquemin's, a lady who, with

her husband, a retired dyer, inhabited a
coquettish little house, ornamented with a
grass plot in front, and a garden at the back,
and situated in the most conspicuous part
of the street.   But notwithstanding these
advantages, M. Jacquemin was an unhappy
man.   He had toiled all his life in order
to enjoy his old age in peace ; and instead of
his fancied happiness, he now found nothing in
retirement save ennui and weariness of spirit. It
was in vain that he spent the day in walking
up and down his handsome house and about
his pleasant garden ; they could administer no
pleasure to his mind.   He would gladly have
given them both for the dark and dismal shop
of the Rue St Denis, where he had spent
thirty years of his life in providing for his present discomfort.   Madame Jacquemin, who
bore her misfortunes with a truly heroic spirit,
endeavoured to arouse her husband from his
unhappy state.   She took him to the play, but
he invariably fell asleep before the close of the
first act; she then wished to introduce him
into fashionable society—a plan which failed
signally ; and finally, as a last resource, made
him take in all the daily newspapers, and give
parties twice a week.   M. Jacquemin never

looked at one of his newspapers himself; but
as he nevertheless, and very judiciously, made
it a rule that not one of them should leave his
house, and as he very liberally invited his
friends to " come and look at the papers," his
salon was every morning converted into a kind
of reading-room, over which he presided, and
where, for two or three hours at least, he could
once more fancy himself in his shop, surrounded by his customers.

His evening parties were not quite so amusing; because, as Madame Jacquemin, often
observed, " they could not ask everybody."
Almost all their guests were inhabitants of the
street; but there were of course vulgar insig-
nificant houses, whose lodgers could, under no
pretence whatever, be received or admitted by
the dyer's wife. Good M. Jacquemin, who,
in the fulness of his ennui, would gladly have
opened his house to the whole world, was
much annoyed by his wife's scruples, but
nevertheless compelled to submit to them.
Amongst the favoured few were M. Bonnet
and his wife, a couple who resided on the first-
floor of number seven, and who, as Madame Legrand, a waspish little widow, who lived above
them, spitefully averred, gave themselves airs in

consequence. But as there was a constant feud between her and Madame Bonnet, too much faith should not be placed in the lady's assertions. M. Bonnet was a melancholy-looking man, exceedingly nervous and timid, and employed at the war-office, whence he often came home in the evening blank with dismay, hinting at horrible tidings from Abd-el-Kader, or intimating the likelihood of a war with "perfidious Albion." Being considered a profound politician, and suspected of knowing much more of government affairs than he chose to tell, he was much respected everywhere, save in his own family, over which Madame Bonnet, who was a very high-spirited woman, boasted that she alone held dominion. Her three daughters were, like their mother, tall, bony, and high-spirited girls.

Madame Legrand, the officer's widow who tenanted the second-floor of the same house, was likewise admitted at the Jacquemin parties. She was thin, withered, had no children, and was immoderately fond of animals. Whole generations of cats and dogs revelled in her salon and bedroom; cages of birds were hung up everywhere in her apartment; and golden fishes swam in vases full of water on every window-sill. Monsieur Laurent, a stout old bachelor, not unlike a full-blown rose, dwelt on the third-floor. He had a mortal hatred against Legrand and her menagerie, those of the canine race in particular. Of this fact the dogs seemed to have an instinctive knowledge, for whenever he came up or down-stairs, they snarled and growled; and if they chanced to be on the landing, never missed the opportunity of flying at his heels. Though Monsieur Laurent disliked animals, he had a passion for flowers and gardening; he had turned his rooms into a perfect conservatory, and the greatest portion of his time was spent in cultivating and watching over a certain patch of land, about as large as a dining-table, and termed his garden. Monsieur Laurent was of course another of Monsieur Jacquemin's invités.

But, besides the inhabitants of number seven, there were various other individuals admitted at the retired dyer's parties. Amongst these were several old ladies, who did an immense quantity of worsted work; and a mysterious family named the De Lorrains, and thought to be of noble extraction, who inhabited an old dreamy-looking hotel at the end of the street.

They were six in all, were very pale, tall, and thin; they dressed meanly, accepted every invitation, and gave none in return. Some charitable souls indeed noticed that they never refused anything, not even the refreshments which were liberally handed round at the dyer's parties; and as to the cakes, it was actually suspected that they were so vulgar and ungenteel as to have an appetite for them. It was also known—it is wonderful how those things are known—that in the coldest weather they had no fires. Sometimes, indeed, they indulged themselves in a fagot, to which they set fire with great ceremony; the youngest De Lorrain being always on such an occasion de-spatched in a great hurry to summon his father, in order that he might partake of the genial heat ere it was quite extinct. At first the De Lorrains were thought mean—then they were accused of being poor; but many de-fended them, and asserted that they were only misers. It then began to be reported that they were immensely rich, and their company was for some time eagerly sought. It is true their fortune, if they had one, was of no great use to anybody, not even to themselves; but who has not felt the sense of security, the

comfort, which lies in having a rich acquaintance? As years, however, passed away, and
they lived quite as meanly, and dressed as
shabbily as ever, this impression wore off:
they began to be looked upon as impostors,
and there was some talk of discarding them
altogether. But Madame Jacquemin, who
was of a compassionate disposition, resolved to
spare them, on account of their poverty and
their gentle blood; they accordingly continued
to be admitted to the soirées, where they acted
a subordinate part, being patronised by every
one. Such were the individuals who met at
M. Jacquemin's parties; if their company did
not afford him much amusement, it was not
their fault. The retired dyer was very selfish:
he plainly showed his visitors that he cared
for no one but himself; yet, strangely enough,
everybody sympathised with him, everybody
seemed ready to administer comfort and
advice.

"If Monsieur Jacquemin would give
dinners," suggested the De Lorrains, "he
would find it a very interesting occupation."

"How so?" suspiciously asked Madame
Jacquemin.

"Human nature, character," replied the De

Lorrains : " the dinner table is the true place to see them in ; physiognomy, too, and even phrenology, can be studied to advantage from the dinner table, and with Monsieur Jacquemin's remarkable power of observation—"

" Pooh, pooh ! no such a thing," interrupted Monsieur Jacquemin, rather crossly, " besides, I hate to look at people eating."

" It is animal," said Madame Legrand, who was present, " and is only beautiful when performed by animals. It is exquisite, it is delicious to see a bird feed."

" I rather like larks roasted," said Monsieur Jacquemin ; " they are nice, there is no doubt about it, but then it takes so many to make a dish."

" My dear sir, you misunderstand me," said Madame Legrand, rather shocked at the suggestion : " eat larks ! sweet, harmonious, musical creatures ! No, no, I meant it was charming to see birds peck their food. I have a canary which I would lend—"

" Oh ! for Heaven's sake, do not mention it," interrupted Madame De Lorrain, with an hysterical laugh, " the screaming little thing would drive Monsieur Jacquemin's head wild."

" Canaries do not scream," said Madame

Legrand, "they sing, but as this one does not sing and has never sung, it could not make Monsieur Jacquemin's head ache."

But Monsieur Jacquemin liked birds in a pie, and peremptorily declined the canary. In this Monsieur Laurent confirmed him.

"Animals, my dear sir," he said feelingly, "would sour your temper, gardening is the thing. You have a garden,—sow, reap, dig, and you will be a happy man. Let me send you down some choice flowers."

"I do not like flowers," growled Monsieur Jacquemin.

Madame Bonnet, too, had her panacea. Why not adopt some interesting and sweet-tempered child; not an orphan—you never know what kind of parents an orphan had; swindlers and thieves perhaps—but a child "whose parents, honest, respectable people, were still alive—and which," she sentimentally added, "would prove the staff and comfort of his old age."

This had nearly settled it. "Old age indeed! did Madame Bonnet think Monsieur Jacquemin was going to make his will? No, no, not just yet. Thank Heaven, he was hale and hearty, and would bury them all."

In short, the plain truth of the matter was that Monsieur Jacquemin liked private dinners best; that he disliked animals, did not care about flowers, and never having had any children of his own, detested the children of other people: Madame Bonnet's included. He felt, besides, all the rich man's aversion to an heir; and constantly refused to see his poor relations, lest they should think of his will.

These were the individuals whom Tancredi P. Mathieu had resolved to civilize, and for that praiseworthy purpose he got an introduction to one of Madame Jacquemin's soirées. At once his eagle eye detected the awful amount of narrow-minded dulness of that little circle. The old ladies were busy at their worsted work; Monsieur Laurent and Madame Legrand were quarrelling over a game of piquet; the melancholy De Lorrains were engaged with dominoes; Monsieur Jacquemin was displaying his hospitality by compelling his guests to swallow down immense quantities of cakes and lemonade; and Monsieur Bonnet sat apart, wrapped in his own moody thoughts, which he occasionally condescended to impart to some eager listener.

" Only a few friends," said Madame Jacquemin, smiling graciously on Tancredi, "a few
homely friends who meet here three times a
week to chat, to talk, to play a few odd
games."

" Squirrels ! " sententiously said Tancredi.

" Squirrels ! " echoed Madame Jacquemin,
amazed.

" Squirrels in a cage," repeated Tancredi,
"turning round and round, doing the same
things over and over again."

" Dear me, how very odd," said Madame
Jacquemin, and raising her voice, she added,
" Monsieur Tancredi Mathieu declares we are
all squirrels."

This strange speech completed the sensation
which Tancredi's long hair, pointed hat, and
white kid gloves had begun. He saw his advantage, and casting a magnetic look—at least
he said so afterwards—over the whole assembly, he followed up this first success with considerable effect.

He scarcely opened his lips, and was
thought a prodigious wit. He seemed to entertain the most thorough contempt for the
whole world, the individuals around him included ; and they all agreed in audible whispers

that he was a very superior sort of person —
quite a genius : great geniuses always despise
the world.   Although both piquet and dominoes were neglected, the evening passed away
with amazing swiftness.   Every one had gathered around the stranger, who opened his mouth
every ten minutes, and delivered some oracular
sentence, received by his hearers with the utmost gravity.

From that day Tancredi P. Mathieu became
the acknowledged lion of the Jacquemin soirées,
and of the Marais, which had never known a
lion before.   He was the object of every one's
admiration : the De Lorrains alone looked
upon him with a suspicious eye ; they had an
instinctive consciousness of a foe.

True, Tancredi did not even bestow a thought
upon them, but, like many remarkable individuals, he showed an early inclination to
tyranny, and betrayed certain destructive pro-
pensities, which threatened to break upon the
quiet monotony of the bourgeois circle.   Being,
as he expressed it himself, of a spiritual nature,
he animadverted in strong terms against the
material custom of eating in the evening.

" Intellectual food is the thing," he loftily
said to Madame Jacquemin.   " Intellectual

food and no other. That alone purifies and exalts."

Madame Jacquemin felt the cogency of this reasoning, and as she considered Tancredi an oracle in matters of taste, she hastened to suppress the refreshments and sweets she had hitherto caused to be freely handed round to her guests.

Having thus victoriously asserted the triumph of mind over matter, Tancredi next succeeded in banishing both piquet and dominoes.

"In no intellectual assembly should such idle toys be admitted," he said to Madame Jacquemin. And piquet and dominoes vanished.

Madame Legrand and Monsieur Laurent, who had quarrelled over the former game for the last twenty years, both loudly protested against this new arrangement, but as their quarrels were only pleasant to themselves, every one agreed that piquet deserved its fate.

Having thus deprived his disciples of their old amusements, our hero felt it his duty to provide them with others in their stead. A piano accordingly made its appearance in Ma-

dame Jacquemin's drawing-room. It is true
nobody could play upon it—not even Tancredi; but that was evidently of little consequence, for towards the close of a very dull
evening he rose, and after vainly beseeching
one of the accomplished ladies present to accompany him, at last sung, unaccompanied,
but still standing near the silent piano, a
pathetic Italian song, in which he bewailed
his unhappy fate; for, as he afterwards con-
descendingly informed the company—who had
not understood a single word—he was a forsaken and despairing lover. After thus initi-
ating them to the charms of melody, Tancredi
resolved to let them into sublimer mysteries,
and accordingly fixed an evening, on which he
proposed to read to Madame Jacquemin's
guests a series of sonnets, which he had composed several years before, " On the Prospect
of being Compelled by my Father to become
a Grocer." This, it must be confessed, was a
little poetical fiction, in which Tancredi had
considered himself at liberty to indulge.
Nothing was ever further from M. Mathieu's
thoughts than to compel his son to anything he
disliked, though he certainly had attempted to

achieve, by persuasion, the profanation above alluded to.

The evening came, the company gathered around him, and Tancredi began his reading: he persevered for upwards of two hours, without manifesting the least symptom of fatigue. When he had finished, he looked up, and found himself alone, comparatively speaking. M. Jacquemin was fast asleep; the old ladies were nodding over their worsted work; Madame Jacquemin had early effected her escape, with several female friends; M. Laurent and M. Bonnet shook their heads, and exchanged ominous glances; the six De Lorrains alone were wide awake, looking at our hero with their fixed stony eyes, whilst their cadaverous and melancholy faces expressed the most absolute determination to sit out both him and his poetry. To increase the dismal appearance of the scene, the fire had gone out, the candles burned dimly, and wanted snuffing, whilst the loud snoring which proceeded from the vast arm-chair in which M. Jacquemin lay, rather marred the melody of the poet's verses. " I see they are not in a sufficiently advanced state of civilization to appreciate the beauties of poetry," thought Tancredi, as he looked upon his audience : " I must form their political principles."

Unfortunately for the execution of this project, it happened that both M. Bonnet and M. Laurent had of late conceived strange notions of Tancredi's political character. His foreign name did not sound quite orthodox in their ear; then his pointed hat, shirt collar, and flowing locks, struck them as being something portentous in their way. Philosophers well know what great meanings sometimes lie hidden under trifles. As to his poetical readings, they had a revolutionary air, in direct opposition to the old school of poetry, and also, they strongly suspected, to the established order of things. Who could tell of whom Tancredi Mathieu might be the agent, or what was going on in the bosom of the hitherto peaceful Marais ? Nay, for all they knew, his pretended Italian love-song might be some revolutionary Marseillaise hymn, or *ça ira*, speciously clothed under a foreign garb ! In short, the employé of the war-office and the horticultural amateur both agreed it was high time to keep their eye upon Tancredi, whom they began to consider as a dangerous political character.

Under these favourable circumstances our hero began his political campaign. He had not yet exactly determined upon the doctrines he meant to inculcate, but he concluded that he would soon find this out; and as he was not a little elated with the success of his previous efforts, he began his attack in the spirit of true knight errantry, dealing out his blows right and left, without much minding where they fell.

"Sir," he said one evening to Monsieur Jacquemin, "this state of things cannot last. Society is wrong, radically wrong. A day will come, sir, when the rich will have to surrender their ill-gotten gold to the poor: and then, beautiful result: there will be no poor and no rich."

"No poor and no rich!" gasped Monsieur Jacquemin, growing purple, "and do you mean to say, sir, that thieves will come and rob me, sir?"

"I make no particular applications of the system," placidly replied Tancredi, "I merely state what will be."

"Well, sir, let them only attempt it," said Monsieur Jacquemin, "let them only try it, ha! ha!—that is all I say."

"'Try it!'" said Monsieur Bonnet, "no, no, they have other work in hand with Abd-el-Kader."

"I admire Abd-el-Kader," thoughtfully ejaculated Tancredi. "He is a hero and a patriot. Besides, what is that puny warfare in Algeria? We shall have a European war before long."

"He admires Abd-el-Kader!" gasped Monsieur Bonnet, unable to say more. Horticulture Tancredi did not, however, admire. He openly expressed his contempt for it to Monsieur Laurent, and plainly said it would be done away with under the new state of things.

"Oh! ho!" said Monsieur Laurent, with a sneer; "and how will the world get on without geraniums or roses? *I* should like to know *that!*"

"Sir," replied Tancredi, with an ominous look, "there are spirits, blighted spirits, for which deadly nightshade, and hemlock itself, have more attractions than all the roses of Syria."

"What a villain!" muttered Monsieur Laurent.

To Madame Legrand Tancredi made no

predictions; but this lady he had long mortally offended beyond all hope of reconciliation, by expressing his ardent desire of seeing every dog hung, and every canary bird shot through the heart; in support of which philanthropic wish he had adduced so many plausible arguments, that the good lady felt convinced that if ever the Young France party prevailed, her menagerie was doomed.

"I know it is Monsieur Laurent's doing," she said to one of the De Lorrains, by whom she was sitting. "I know that man—"

A fearful scream interrupted her. One of the old ladies had gone into fits, and this was no sooner perceived by the other old ladies, her friends, than, out of mere sympathy, they followed her example. Awful was the confusion that followed; Madame Jacquemin was pretty well frightened out of her wits; Tancredi, who had caused all this hubbub, stood and looked on, smiling and triumphant.

"Good Heavens! what has happened?" exclaimed Madame Legrand. One of the De Lorrains rose to learn, and soon came back with the tidings.

"Dreadful!" she said. "You know Mademoiselle du Rocher's family were all guillotined in the terror? "

" Well! " eagerly exclaimed Madame Legrand.

" Well, this wretch goes up to her and says : ' Madame, do you know that I am wonderfully like Robespierre? ' Upon which the poor thing looks at him, and perceiving the likeness, screams and faints."

" Monster ! " said Madame Legrand. She spoke loud enough for Tancredi to hear. He acknowledged the epithet with a gracious smile, and left the place at Madame Jacquemin's request.

" If she sees you," said that lady, " she will certainly relapse. Pray go."

Tancredi left delighted with this crowning exploit. With this tact and discrimination did he endeavour to civilize the bourgeois of the Marais : the succession of petty storms and alarms he raised must be left to the imagination of the reader. It is true that, had the worthy citizens known anything about either Tancredi P. Mathieu, or the Young France party, they would have been conscious that the former was the most harmless of human beings, and from the latter there was little or

nothing to be apprehended. The Young
France party, with their kid gloves and hair
carefully curled, were no doubt the fit apostles
of a revolution, but by such revolutions are
not generally made. But fear reasons not:
Tancredi's words were received as gospel
truth, and pretty work they soon made in the
Marais.

The dragon's teeth were not sown in vain:
quarrels sprung on every side. Madame Bonnet took it into her head to sympathise with
Abd-el-Kader, who became the subject of daily
dissentions between her and her husband. A
new and deadly feud sprang up beween Monsieur Laurent and Madame Legrand, the former of whom avowed that in consequence of
Tancredi's disastrous teaching, his finest
flower-beds were ruined by the widow's dogs.
Rendered desperate by one of those melancholy events, and recalling to mind Tancredi's
denunciations against pets of every description, Monsieur Laurent, having provided himself with tackle and a fishing-rod, exercised
his vengeance on one of Madame Legrand's
unoffending golden fishes, by actually fishing
it up through his bed-room window. The
unhappy lady, who, hearing a suspicious noise

against the highest window panes, had rushed
to the rescue, only arrived in time to see her
finny favourite whisked up in the air, and
vanishing into the enemy's precincts. Her
first act was to snatch in her remaining trea-
sures, who, quite unconscious of their companion's fate, were still gaily swimming along their
narrow domain; the next was to scream for
help, and then faint away in good earnest.
When she recovered, she found herself surrounded by condoling friends ; but nothing
could soothe her wounded spirit. She declared that she never should forgive M. Laurent, against whom she vowed eternal hatred
and vengeance.

But even greater evils—all springing from
the same source—menaced the guests of M.
Jacquemin. The worthy dyer, on whom Tancredi's speeches had made a profound impression, began to entertain serious fears for his
safety. Lest his reputation of being a
wealthy man should bring him into trouble,
he determined to reduce his expenditure ; and,
as a first step, talked of discontinuing to take
in the daily papers, and stopping the soirées
altogether. This announcement spread a
panic throughout the whole street. M. Jac-

quemin's house had become a place of public
entertainment, which his guests had no inclination to find closed upon them. In this
dilemma a general council was held; private
dissensions were for a while forgotten, and it
was unanimously resolved to strike at the root
of the evil, and banish Tancredi P. Mathieu.
The gaunt De Lorrains, who alone had from
the beginning perceived the impending danger, proposed to signalize him to the mayor of
the arrondissement as a dangerous individual;
M. Bonnet offered to say a few words at the
war-office; M. Laurent to give him a delicate
hint in the language of flowers; Madame Legrand proposed a night attack on his person;
and the old ladies were for handling him over
to the public executioner at once. But Madame Jacquemin rejected all these plans as too
violent and inhospitable, and resolved to inti-
mate to him, as politely as possible, that if he
chose to continue his visits, it must no longer
be on his own terms, but on hers. Accordingly, when Tancredi came as usual to one of
the evening soirées, his head full of mighty
plans of poetical, social, and political reform,
he could not, notwithstanding his abstrac-
tion, but notice that a great change had taken

place. The piano, which had only been hired for a month, had vanished; M. Laurent and Madame Legrand were quarrelling over piquet to their heart's content; the De Lorrains, who were eating cakes and drinking lemonade, eyed him with defiance; dominoes were reëstablished in their supremacy; and the old ladies were as triumphantly engaged in worsted-work as on the night of his first appearance amongst them.

One glance told Tancredi that the bourgeois of the Marais had rebelled: his authority was no longer acknowledged; he was virtually dethroned. Even the most energetic minds must sometimes yield to the might of fate: thus it was with our hero. Vanquished, but unsubdued in spirit, he nevertheless saw the uselessness of resistance. Casting a glance of withering scorn on his late disciples, he spake not a word, but turned upon his heel, and left the drawing-room of Madame Jacquemin, inwardly passing the fatal fiat, "for ever." With signal ingratitude, every one uttered an exclamation of triumph on witnessing his exit. The remainder of the evening was spent in perfect enjoyment—harmony seemed quite restored; and it is averred

that, notwithstanding the late painful circumstances that had occurred, the quarrels of M.
Laurent and the fair widow were marked by
unusual amenity.

The day after his defeat, Tancredi wrote
to Charlemagne Champion a letter of seven
pages, in which he related, with great seeming bitterness of spirit, his vain attempt to
civilize a parcel of barbarians, and instil
into their uncultivated minds a love of the
fine arts, and a sound political creed. He
ended by exclaiming against the cruelty of
mankind, that would not allow him one
moment's repose; and as he had little
doubt that the malice of his antagonists
would drive them to every extremity, spoke
of exiling himself in some remote solitude,
where his wounded spirit might perhaps
at last find rest!

By return of post he received the following answer:

" Dear Tancredi,

" I am by no means astonished at your
failure; you have met with a fate common to
all great spirits; you ought not, therefore, to
mourn, but to rejoice. Had you, however,
consulted me on the subject, I could have

foretold exactly what has happened. Whatever you do, never again attempt to civilize
bourgeois. They are very worthy people
in their way, but singularly obstinate. They
like to enjoy themselves according to their
own stupid old-fashioned manner. As they
are fast disappearing from the surface of
the land, it is only an act of mercy to
allow them to live unmolested. Henceforth
heed them not, but turn all your efforts
and energies on the rising generation. Give
up the thought of going into exile; talents
like yours should not be wasted away in
a desert.

"Your devoted

"CHARLEMAGNE CHAMPION."

But Tancredi was bent on being a persecuted man, and once in his life, at least,
an exile. He announced to his father his
intention of leaving the country for some
time. Monsieur Mathieu the elder heard
him with much more composure than, from
the painful nature of the communication,
might have been expected ; he even remarked that travelling would do his son
good, and seemed to view the whole affair
as one of minor importance. It was in

vain that Tancredi endeavoured to impress
upon his mind that he was going to leave
his country perhaps for ever. Monsieur
Mathieu persisted in asserting that he was
only going to travel, and very calmly bade
him farewell.

In a few days Tancredi left Paris for
Geneva. We will not dwell on the agonizing nature of his feelings when, having
passed the frontier, he beheld from the
diligence window the blue hills of his
country—his native hills, as, forgetting his
Parisian birth, he called them—vanish from
his view. For three months he wandered
on the shores of Lake Leman, and indulged
in misanthropic reflections on the folly and
ingratitude of mankind. At the expiration
of that term—during which he had been,
to say the truth, the prey to intolerable
ennui—he gladly hastened back to Paris,
without, however, informing his father of
his intention. On a fine summer evening
he bent his steps towards his father's house
in the Marais: he still wore his pointed
hat, and a travelling cloak enveloped his
person; a porter who followed him carried
his luggage. Without allowing himself to

be announced, Tancredi, who loved dramatic effect, rushed into the parlour, where his father was seated reading the newspaper, and throwing back his cloak, discovered himself to the ex-grocer's astonished sight. Good Monsieur Mathieu laid down the paper instantly, and uttered a very deep hem; but as he was not what is called a very nervous man, he did not seem otherwise affected, but kindly welcomed his son; and seeing that he looked as rosy and happy as ever, immediately gave orders for a substantial supper. Tancredi, who was rapturously gazing through the window on the starlit sky of his native city, of course heard or heeded nothing of those material concerns; " his spirit was far away."

"Well, Pierre, how did you like Geneva?" asked Monsieur Mathieu, turning towards his son, whom he never called Tancredi.

" All places are alike; he is everywhere alone," moodily answered his son in the words of Lamennais.

M. Mathieu, who saw that Tancredi was still bent on being wretched, remained silent, and took up his newspaper once more.

" I suppose," resumed Tancredi after a

brief pause, "the malignancy of their hatred is unabated ? "

" Of whom are you speaking? " inquired his father with seeming surprise.

" Of M. Jacquemin, his wife, and all those whose ingratitude made me fly my native land."

" Oh, they are very well, thank you ; they were all inquiring after you only last week."

" I know they hate me ; yet I wish them no evil," replied Tancredi, with the resignation of a martyr. " I earnestly hope they are happy ? "

" They are indeed quite happy," answered his father.

Tancredi smiled incredulously. " How can they be happy," he exclaimed, " when they are a prey to all the evil passions that disturb mankind ? I endeavoured to reclaim and civilize them ; I failed in the attempt, but I cannot think them happy ! "

" Well," said his father, quietly, " since you went to Geneva I have seen a good deal more of them : I at first found them much irritated against you."

"Ha! I knew it!" triumphantly exclaimed Tancredi.

"But I soon succeeded in pacifying them," continued his father, without heeding the interruption. Tancredi looked as though he could have gladly dispensed with this in-stance of paternal solicitude.

"I, moreover, tried to make them happy; not perhaps according to the best manner, but according to that best suited to them."

Tancredi's features expressed unqualified surprise: he seemed to wait for something else, but his father remaining silent, he at last said: "Well, sir, I suppose, by making them happy, you mean making them better?" M. Mathieu nodded affirmatively. "If so," continued his son, "pray how did you rid M. Jacquemin of his intolerable selfishness and sordid love of wealth?"

"M. Jacquemin," quietly answered the father, "is, as you say, selfish, and fond of money; but he is no miser: he has no objection to spend large sums, provided it is to please himself. Had I advised him, as you did, to divide the wealth he did not need amongst the poor, he would have looked upon me as a madman. When he

complained to me of his great ennui, I advised him to settle in business some of his
poor nephews and nieces, whom he had
always refused to see, lest they should expect anything from him. He at first seemed
very much opposed to this plan; but when
I reminded him that after his death his
fortune must belong to his relations, who
would perhaps squander it away, and that
it would be more pleasant for him to dispose of it, according to his own fancy,
during his lifetime, he quite agreed with
me, and immediately took steps to place
his eldest nephew in a dyer's business,
which he takes great delight in superintend-
ing. He has likewise provided for his
other relations, with whom he occasionally
quarrels, but towards whom he, nevertheless, behaves with much real kindness. He
still takes in the papers, and has not dis-
continued the soirées; but as he now has
little leisure, he is glad to lend out the
former to his friends, and enjoys the relax-
ation of the latter much more than formerly : he is, upon the whole, a happier and
a better man."

" Humph!" almost contemptuously exclaimed Tancredi. "I had embraced all humanity in my plan; yours, I perceive, is confined to making a few persons happy."

"It is at least the more practicable of the two," replied his father.

"And I suppose," continued Tancredi, "that you also succeeded in reconciling M. Laurent and Madame Legrand; who, with their insufferable love of flowers, and animals, and mutual antipathy, were enough to destroy all harmony wherever they appeared?"

"I did not endeavour to reconcile them," answered M. Mathieu; "but when M. Laurent informed me of all he had to suffer from his neighbour the widow, I advised him to marry her, upon which he told me in confidence that he had been thinking of it for the last ten years, and without waiting for a reply, launched out into her praises. In short, it ended by his requesting me to be the bearer of a letter to her, as he averred that he could not summon up courage to address her himself. I consented to undertake this task. On reading the letter, which was a very long one, Madame Legrand became greatly agitated, said something about a golden fish, but at last declared that she forgave him everything."

"But they are not actually married!" exclaimed Tancredi.

"They have been so for the last six weeks," replied M. Mathieu.

"And do you mean to say," asked his son, "that they no longer quarrel?"

"On the contrary, they quarrel every day; but as it may be safely asserted that it is more from the force of habit than from any other motive, they can be said to agree very well upon the whole. Very little is changed in their existence. They live in the same house; Madame Laurent still occupies the second-floor with her animals, and M. Laurent the third with his flowers; they enjoy their game of piquet, and its accompanying squabble, every evening; and it is my firm belief that their greatest cause of complaint against you was the attempt you made to deprive them of that pleasure."

Tancredi turned up his eyes to the ceiling, and in a tone full of indignation, began, "Who will attempt to fathom the duplicity of man? Who—" Here he became suddenly silent, either overwhelmed by the vastness of the subject of his question, or induced to hold his peace by the aspect of the supper on the table.

Several days elapsed before Tancredi could be induced to accompany his father on a visit to M. Jacquemin. He at last expressed his consent, by declaring himself "ready to face his enemies." His father, who had learned to understand his enigmatical mode of speech, required no more. They accordingly called on the retired dyer the same evening: the Bonnets, Laurents, and De Lorrains, were all present; they seemed delighted to see our hero, and received him with the greatest cordiality. When his father commented on this circumstance, Tancredi smiled bitterly, and muttered something about the serpent being hidden by flowers. But the truth was, that since M. Mathieu had given M. Jacquemin's guests to understand that his son's mind had been somewhat disturbed by certain visions, prevalent amongst the youth of France, their anger had been turned into pity, which they now openly expressed. But of this Tancredi saw, or would see, nothing: they had hated him three months back, they must hate him still; and with this

soothing unction to his wounded pride, he endeavoured to comfort himself.

Several years have elapsed, and no important
change has occurred in the bosom of the little
society we have attempted to portray. M.
Jacquemin has forgotten the name of ennui
since he followed his friend M. Mathieu's
advice; his poor relations are in a thriving
condition, and seem to feel much gratitude for
his kindness. M. Bonnet still menaces his
friends with an impending European war; but
it has been noticed that they have now become
quite accustomed to the prediction. Madame
Bonnet, whose thoughts are all bent on matrimonial alliances for her daughters, has entirely
forgotten Abd-el-Kader. M. and Madame
Laurent quarrel less every day; it is strongly
suspected by their friends that the time will
come at last when they will not quarrel at all!
The only great event which has occurred concerns the De Lorrains; it seems that, after all,
they were immensely rich. A law-suit, which
lasted for several years, had prevented them
from entering into the enjoyment of their
fortune. The old hotel is shut up: its inhabitants have removed to a fashionable neighbourhood, where they live in style, and keep

their carriage. Circumstances have wonderfully altered their outward appearance. They
all have quite a bold and prosperous air.
They frequently invite their former patrons to
their parties; but either the Jacquemin set are
hurt at the long deception practised upon
them, or they have not yet made up their
minds to forgive the De Lorrains their sudden
and unexpected prosperity; for, with the exception of the first invitation, which they only
accepted out of curiosity, they have declined
all other requests, taking in high dudgeon the
splendour of the entertainment offered to them.
It is, nevertheless, suspected that they will
relent in time, if not for their own sakes, at
least for that of their children, to whom, as
Madame Bonnet observes, they will, of course,
feel desirous of securing the comfort of a rich
acquaintance. But Madame Laurent, who
still entertains a grudge against her neighbour,
declares that she has other designs on the De
Lorrains, and is determined to keep her eye
upon her. We must not forget to record that
several of the old ladies have been cut away
by the remorseless hand of death. It is
worthy of notice, that those who still survive
have never been able to forget Tancredi's un-

lucky likeness to Marat; they evidently look upon this circumstance as very suspicious.

This brings us naturally to our hero. Of him we have very little to say. He is, to all appearance, as rosy, and happy-looking, and miserable in reality as ever. His father, nevertheless, asserts that he has of late manifested symptoms of change. His hat is not quite so pointed, his shirt collar is no longer Byronian, and his hair has actually been cropped quite close by the neighbouring hairdresser, who declares that he only followed his positive orders. But what looks more ominous still is, that the name of Tancredi has vanished from his cards, which now only bear plain P. Mathieu. Whatever may be the causes of this change—and whether it is to be attributed to his failure in not being able to become a persecuted man, or whether there is some other motive for it—it seems, nevertheless, very probable that a crisis in P. Mathieu's character is at hand. Some persons have been found who begin to think, like his father, that he may, after all, settle down into a sober, sensible individual: a supposition the more probable, that he actually has been heard to talk of marrying and entering into business; and that, after all, his youthful follies were more fit subjects for good-humoured ridicule than for real apprehension—a remark which many individuals have actually applied to the Young France party itself.

ADRIEN.

In a gloomy and winding street of the cité there stands an old crazy-looking house seven stories high, which appears to have been most uncomfortably squeezed and narrowed up by its more modern neighbours, and has upon the whole an insecure and tottering air. The gate of this house, as in all the poorer dwellings, stands ever open for the convenience of the numerous lodgers; beyond it extends a low cellar-like arch, which terminates with a glimpse of an old pump in a damp, grass-grown yard; on the left of the arch exists a dark hole—the lodge wherein dwells a cross old portress, who has, not unnaturally, contracted a dark and misanthropical view of the world. Night and day a lamp is always burning in that lodge, whilst a dull, glimmering ray of light, descending from a high and remote window, reveals the winding staircase which leads to the various floors of the house.

It was in a garret, situated on the last of
these seven stories, that there lived, a few
years ago, an orphan lad named Adrien, and
his grandmother, an old weak-minded peasant
woman, who still appeared as great a stranger
to Paris and Parisian life as when she entered
for the first time the capital of France. To
the humble abode of this obscure couple we
will now introduce the reader. The room was
indeed a mere garret, scarcely more than
eight feet square, with low ceiling and slanting
walls; but though narrow and bare, it was
neat and clean. The *lit de sangle*, or framed
canvass, so common amongst those of the
Parisian poor who cannot afford room for a
bedstead, was folded up with its thin mattress
against the wall; the lame deal table had
been most scrupulously scrubbed; no dust or
stain appeared on the red-tiled flooring; a
few battered kitchen utensils which hung on
the walls were placed with a sort of regard to
symmetry; a piece of broken looking-glass
adorned the mantel-shelf; near it was suspended a five sous portrait of Napoleon, under which
had been placed, as if in homage, a blooming
pot of the modest flower known amongst us as

the mignonette, but which in France is
generally called réséda. A golden sunbeam
which streamed in through the narrow and
open window, and fell on the little broken
mirror, brightened the whole place with its
joyous and cheerful light.

Near that window now sat in a rickety
arm-chair Adrien's grandmother, attired in her
peasant's dress of short and striped woollen
petticoat, blue jacket, and headgear consisting
of a printed calico kerchief. Without expressing either ill health or physical infirmity, the
old woman's sunburnt features betrayed a
mental helplessness, painful to behold as she
sat there with her hands folded on her knees,
watching listlessly every motion of her active
grandson. With his shrewd intelligent
countenance, dark curly hair, and well knit,
though diminutive frame, he was only fifteen,
Adrien offered a very favourable specimen of
the Parisian gamin. The confident bearing,
decisive attitudes, and frank good-humoured
accent, revealed at once a true son of Paris.
The lad was now in a state of great bustle and
preparation—lighting a charcoal fire, heating a
pan over it, melting dripping, peeling onions,

singing snatches of songs in spite of his smarting eyes, throwing the onions into the pan
when the dripping had reached frying heat,
and, in short, preparing that favourite French
dish—onion soup, which ere long was smoking
on the table in an old earthenware tureen.

"Come, grandmother," said Adrien, in a
cheerful tone, "breakfast is ready;" and he
closed his eyes and smacked his lips as he
inhaled the curling vapour which rose from
his plate. "How rich it looks," he added,
admiringly. "Upon my word of honour, I
know nothing better for a working man than a
dish of onion soup."

The old woman, without seeming to share
his enthusiasm, cast a dreary look on the dark
liquid, and partook of it very slowly. Not
even the manly, swaggering tone with which
Adrien concluded his speech had power to
rouse her. It is true she was accustomed to
it. When they first began to live together a
few months before, she had indeed wondered
with a dreamy sort of perplexity on whose side
the mistake lay, when she thought Adrien a
boy, and he evidently considered himself a
man; but his cool, decisive manner had
promptly laid the matter at rest, and she

would now as soon have dreamed of doubting her own identity, as of questioning his authority and experience.

" Well, what shall we have for dinner? " said Adrien, who had finished his soup, and, balancing himself back on his chair with his hands thrust into his pockets, was now watching the old woman.

" Let us have a stew of mutton and haricots, Adrien," she promptly replied.

" Grandmother," said he, impressively, " I only earn six francs (five shillings) a week."

" Well then a cabbage soup, with a good piece of bacon in it."

" Bacon is horribly dear ; but if you like the cabbage without it—"

" No, I don't," was the snappish answer.

" I should propose sorrel soup," continued Adrien, " but it is no good without eggs, which we cannot afford ; or bean soup if we had only got beans, which we have not. Do you know," he confidentially added, " that we have some dripping," his eyes fell on an earthen pot standing in the corner of the room, " and plenty of onions," he glanced at a bunch hanging from a nail on the wall ; " do you know I think we could not do better than to have a good, hot, smoking tureenful of onion soup."

"Onion soup!" indignantly exclaimed the old woman; "why we have had onion soup all the week; Adrien," she pathetically added, "do you mean to say we must live on onion soup?" Adrien looked embarrassed, but he resolutely replied:

"Yes, grandmother, we must—if we cannot help it."

"Onion soup made with dripping, too," she mournfully added, rocking herself to and fro, "and never even a drop of wine."

"Grandmother," observed her grandson, very gravely, and pausing in his task of clearing away the breakfast things, "you *know* Paris wine gives you the headache. You remember," he added, in a lower tone, "how strangely you behaved when that wicked Madame Mitron, next door, persuaded you to go with her to the barrier. No, no, wine is not good for *you*. It excites you," said he, after seeming at a loss for the proper word, "it excites you."

"And to live in such a garret!" she continued, without heeding him.

"Garret!" he echoed, glancing admiringly

round him; "why, have you not a good warm bed?"

"Yes, Adrien, but you sleep on the floor."

"I prefer it," he hastily replied; "it is more wholesome, you see. And then," he resumed, "have you not got a portrait of the Emperor, and a looking-glass, and a pot of réséda, and the sun that comes in every morning; and always plenty of bread and soup to eat?"

"Onion soup, Adrien."

"Add to which advantage," said Adrien, summing up, "that you have nothing to do but to walk about Paris all day long, or, if you prefer staying at home, to look out of the window and enjoy yourself."

"And look at the smoky chimney-pots," replied the old woman, despondingly.

"Grandmother, I wonder at you! You know that you have only to place the table near the window — mind the broken foot though—and put a chair on the table, and get up on the chair yourself, in order to have the finest view possible of the towers of Notre Dame."

But a prospect of the Paris cathedral, though thus obtained, did not seem to com-

fort Adrien's old relative. She did not like
Notre Dame; it was too large and gloomy;
she wanted the little, white, sunny church of
her own village; she wanted that village itself,
with its comfortable dwellings and well-stored
larders, and abundance of all good things.
Paris was a drear, dismal place, and Paris she
would leave.

"Impossible," interposed Adrien. "In the
first place, you know you have no one to go
back to in your own village, as you call it;
but even if you had," he added, with an important air, "I could not allow you to go."

The old woman looked up quite bewildered.
"You do not mean to say, Adrien, that you
would keep me here against my will?"

"Yes, I do. Come," said he, sitting down
by her, and speaking with sudden gravity,
"you know—for you were by—and it is not
long ago, what my poor father said to me on
his death-bed, 'Adrien, my boy,' said he, 'I
am going away; God bless you; be an honest
working man; pay your way and take care of
your poor old grandmother.' Now," observed
Adrien, after a little pause, "an honest working man I believe I am; my way I have paid
till now; we are not like old Madame Mitron,

who drinks all she has, never pays her rent,
and looks another way when she passes before
the sour old portress's lodge; we can look the
landlord himself straight in the face, grandmother; but that is not all, and I should not
have done my father's will if I did not take
care of you; so you see you must remain with
me. After all I do earn six francs a week."

"You are a good lad, Adrien," exclaimed
his grandmother, sobbing and throwing her
arms around his neck in a sudden revulsion of
feeling.

"Nay," said he, with gravity, "I only do
my duty as an honest man, you know."

By this time it was getting late; and, as
Adrien said, quite time for him to be gone to
his work. But whilst completing his pre-
parations — for he was extremely neat and
careful of his person—he undertook to administer consolations to his grandmother,
whose tears were still flowing.

"Come, grandmother, don't cry, we all
have our troubles. If you knew what we car-
penters have to endure; and if one happens to
be short, what advantage is taken of it. Look
at that Grand Jean, who, because he is six
foot high, cannot meet one on the staircase

without talking of tom-tits. Ah, grandmother, if it were not for you—," and a significant and ominous frown gathered over the boy's smooth brow as he spoke.

"Holy virgin!" screamed the old woman, "you don't think, Adrien, of attacking that big, tall man?"

"No, indeed, I do not," gravely answered her grandson; "I hope I know my duty to you better. Why, suppose Jean and I were to have an affair, and I to hit him, and hurt him, I should certainly be sent to prison; and then," he pathetically added, "then, what would become of you?" Adrien seemed overwhelmed with emotion at the idea. But he was now quite ready; so slinging his basket of tools over his shoulder, he embraced his grandmother, and hesitatingly observed, "if old Madame Mitron should try and lure you to the barrier, grandmother, you will not go?"

"No," she slowly replied.

"You know," he said, colouring as he alluded to his old relative's secret infirmity, "that wine excites you. I shall be back at two," he continued, after a pause, "so pray try and have the onion soup ready."

The name of this unlucky dish immediately brought a cloud over the old woman's brow, and as he closed the door, Adrien heard her muttering " onion soup ! " indignantly.

Scarcely had Adrien issued on the landing, when a door opposite gently opened, and afforded him a glimpse of a very red and pimpled face. " So old Mitron wants to see me out before she begins her tricks with poor grandmother," thought Adrien. Madame Mitron, seeing herself discovered, no longer affected concealment, and nodding at Adrien, with what he considered a most insolent familiarity, for he was apt to be wonderfully ticklish on small points of dignity, cavalierly addressed him with a " Bonjour, Adrien."

" Bonjour, Madame," he loftily replied ; " allow me to observe that you might say, Monsieur Adrien."

" Pray, how long have we called ourselves Monsieur Adrien ? " she asked, with a sneer ; and Madame Mitron burst into a fit of laughter which shook her dropsical frame. " Very amusing," she observed, when her merriment was over; and she clapped the door in his face. Adrien disliked Madame Mitron, and not without a cause ; "she was always," he

said, "endeavouring to corrupt his innocent
grandmother, luring her to the barrier, where
she got excited with adulterated wine." He
was sure his grandmother was no drunkard ;
she was only new to Paris, and to the neces-
sity of living on six francs a week. If she
would only believe *him* when he assured her
they were very comfortable upon the whole.
But she would persist in preferring butter to
dripping, meat to onion soup, and wine to
water ! Foolish grandmother ! But he loved
her for all that, and even with a sort of pride ;
she has been very handsome, he often thought,
as he looked admiringly at her sunburnt and
wrinkled features, where to no other eyes
would a trace of beauty have been visible.
Then on a Sunday, when she donned her
holiday gear, and they went out together, how
he admired her with her high white cap, the
gold cross suspended from her neck, and the
short and full petticoat of flaring pattern.
They might have been so happy, but for Madame Mitron ; why did that weak grandmother yield to her wicked advice and entrust
her with a gold cross and little articles of
country finery, which, through her agency,
were speedily converted into barrier banquets ?

And to think that, after causing all this mischief, Madame Mitron should presume to insult him!

This was not destined to be Adrien's only
tribulation on this unlucky morning; at a turn
of the staircase he suddenly found himself face
to face with Grand Jean. Grand Jean was a
big, heavy, good-tempered working man, a
native of the mountains of Auvergne, who resided in the same house with Adrien; the
lad's pretensions to equality seemed to afford
him infinite amusement whenever they met,
but when fiery little Adrien attempted to annoy
and provoke him in his turn, the colossal Jean
evidently considered the joke rich beyond
description. He now gave him a good-
humoured nod and smile, for he liked the
lad in his heart, and greeted him with, "and
how are *we* getting on this fine morning,
Adrien?"

"Very well," replied Adrien, in a sharp
tone, and with a peculiarly defiant jerk of his
head; "please to allow me to pass," he im-
peratively added, for the burly form of Jean
obstructed the narrow staircase.

"Of course," said Jean; and, without standing on one side, he raised his arm horizontally,

apparently intimating that Adrien was welcome to pass underneath it. Truth compels us to declare that he could have done so without the greatest inconvenience.

"Sir!" said Adrien, colouring to the very temples.

"So we are getting in a pet, as usual," benignantly remarked Grand Jean, making room for him, and gently patting him on the head as he spoke.

"Sir!" cried Adrien, in a shriller tone, and pulling his cap over his eyebrows, for he was perfectly exasperated; but Jean, with provoking indifference and good-humour, continued to ascend the staircase, merely turning round to give Adrien a last friendly nod as he vanished from his sight.

"It is better to bear it quietly, for the sake of grandmother," heroically observed Adrien to himself; but he swallowed the affront very unwillingly, and considered himself an extremely ill-used individual. And, indeed, was he quite fairly treated? Left on his own resources whilst still a boy, he had to support himself and his old relative; nay, even to control her conduct, and assume all the duties and responsibilities of a man; but he was

expected to do this without taking any of the
state and dignity of the character he had to
sustain. Fortunately for Adrien, he did not
behold the matter in this light. His self-
delusion with regard to his own importance
was without the alloy of a doubt, and he
ascribed to individual perverseness the occasional mortifications he endured. But as these
mortifications were highly unpleasant, and as
the best of us must occasionally indulge in
some trifling weakness, Adrien, in order to
soothe his wounded pride, now thought fit to
pause before the misanthropical portress's
lodge—that dark hole where the lamp, like the
sacred fire on the altar of Vesta, was kept ever
burning; and, thrusting in his head, to observe
with a condescending nod and gracious smile:
"And how are *we* getting on to-day, Mère
Moreau?"

The old portress, who was skimming her
soup near the fire, looked up with mute surprise, and for one moment the ladle paused in
its office; but before she could recover from
the amazement into which this audacious intrusion had thrown her, Adrien vanished.
This little ebullition of vanity restored him at
once to his usual equanimity of temper. He

left the dingy old house, singing like a lark, and went down the winding street in the best possible humour with himself and the whole world.

At two exactly the gay little Adrien reäppeared under the cellar-like arch, and he was hastening up the gloomy staircase with his light and buoyant step, when the cracked voice of Madame Moreau called him back. He turned round and beheld that lady's thin visage scowling at him from the entrance of the dark hole where she spent her life. "Here is the key of your room," she sharply said.

"Is grandmother out?" he falteringly asked, as he took the key.

"Yes, she is, and with Madame Mitron too!" and giving Adrien a look of resentful defiance, the portress vanished in her den. Adrien slowly ascended the staircase. How changed now looked the empty room. No neatly-laid table with the hot smoking soup awaited him after his hard morning's work. The poor lad looked around him, sat down, and bowing his face between his hands, fairly wept. Of what use did it seem for him to work so hard, to be frugal and thrifty beyond his years, to save and stint in order to live on the six francs a week, to come home with his light cheerful bearing. His grandmother was gone, disgracing herself—disgracing him. When or how would she come back ? This last thought was indeed a thought of terror; the young are keenly alive to disgrace. Adrien believed that his grandmother's indiscretions had until now escaped notice; every one in the house knew of them, but with the native delicacy of French politeness, all feigned perfect unconsciousness; even cross old Mère Moreau spared the lad's sensitive pride. " How cleverly I must have managed to smuggle her in," he often thought, with secret exultation; and when he gave a sigh to his old relative's errors, he reflected, like Francis I. after the battle of Pavia, that honour at least was safe. But if an exposure should take place now. Oh ! then he must leave the house instantly—nay, the neighbourhood itself, and dim visions of quitting Paris altogether even floated across his brain. Adrien was too sad to prepare onion soup, so he dined on bread and dripping. Madame Moreau noticed his altered bearing and inflamed eyes, though he turned his head away, as he handed her the key on going down; she took, or rather snatched it from him with her usual surliness, but her heart was touched at the lad's evident sorrow.

Amongst the habits of this lady (who had many) was that of emerging from her lodge towards twilight, like a night bird, in order to spend the fine summer evenings on the step of the street door. From this tribunal of her misanthropy she philosophically surveyed the world, her arms defiantly folded on her breast, her head inclined towards her right shoulder, in mournful contemplation of human follies,—her whole attitude expressive of supreme disdain. A scornful sneer lit up her solemn features on these occasions, and bitterly sarcastic remarks fell from her lips. These remarks were not narrowly confined to peculiar subjects, or directed to certain individuals. Attacks on government, with Madame Moreau's own suggestions, sneers at rival portresses over the way, lamb-like complaints of her own private wrongs, hints to ungrateful lodgers, who might regret her when she was dead and gone, mingled with sudden and fierce apostrophes directed towards unconscious and inoffensive passengers, formed the staple of discourses addressed to the world in general,

but of which the lodgers, who constantly came
in and out at this hour, derived the full benefit.
And much did they dread these evening objur-
gations in which, with her. broken, half-
abstracted manner, Madame Moreau contrived
to disclose to the public their most private
concerns. If Monsieur B. ill-used his wife,
the portress railed at the men straightway, and
with singular generosity she only became the
more explicit in her narrative if there happened
to exist any little difference between herself
and Madame B.

His knowledge of this touching peculiarity
increased Adrien's apprehensions as he came
home in the evening. What if the old woman
had returned, and Madame Moreau, mindful
of the morning, should pity him aloud for
having a drunken grandmother! Oh, that
there were only a back door! But there was
none; and standing in awful majesty on the
threshold of the arch, with a group of lodgers
listening to her, he beheld Madame Moreau.
He took courage, however, and assuming a
disengaged air, addressed the portress with a
remark concerning the fineness of the weather.
She gave him a sour look that implied, "Do
not imagine you can cheat or deceive me;"

but she merely said, " Sir, your key is hanging
on a nail in the lodge."

Adrien sighed to learn that his grandmother
had not yet returned; but with all that, he
felt grateful for the old portress's forbearance.
It was a sad evening for the lad, as he sat in
the dark, stepping out on the landing every
five minutes, peeping down the well-like staircase, listening anxiously when a knock was
heard below, and feeling his heart leap up to
his mouth every time the street door opened
and closed again. Deceived by the step of
other lodgers, he thought two or three times
the truant was returned; a solemn moral
reproof rose to his lips; nay, he would feign
sleep and perfect indifference. But none of
the steps ascended the seventh story, and every
time his illusion vanished Adrien's sorrow came
back. The house had long been silent, when,
towards eleven, he heard a weak and tottering
footstep. " It is only the lodger below,"
thought he, anxious not to deceive himself.
But the staircase creaked, the step continued
to ascend, it stopped on the landing, and a
light gleamed through the chink of his door.
Adrien opened it, and saw Madame Mitron;
she was alone.

" Where is grandmother ? " he hastily exclaimed.

" Don't know," she thickly replied, endeavouring to open her door.

" You shall not go in ; where is she ? " cried Adrien, placing himself before her.

" I tell you I do not know," testily replied the old woman. " We went to the barrier for a walk, had a salad, a glass of wine, and were coming home, when a crowd divided us at the end of the Pont-Neuf. A child had been run over ; people said it was not hurt ; but I had got such a turn, that I was obliged to take five or six glasses of brandy at a grocer's before I could get over it."

" So," indignantly said Adrien, " you lured away my weak, innocent grandmother—the poor thing would never go to the barrier— and then abandoned her, when she does not know one street from another, and may get into any mischief. God forgive you ! " he mournfully added, as he turned away, with heart too full for more bitter reproach.

" God forgive me ! you good-for-nothing little scamp," screamed Madame Mitron with sudden rage, her eyes well nigh starting out of her head, as she shook her candlestick at

Adrien. "God forgive me! How dare you
hint at such a thing, you mite, you—"

The rest was lost upon Adrien, who hastily
descended the staircase, heedless of her
drunken railings.

"Monsieur Adrien, if you think I am going
to sit up for *you*," wrathfully observed the old
portress, as he swiftly passed by her lodge;
but the door being half open, he had reached
the street before the end of her sentence.
He went straight to the Pont-Neuf; the acci-
dent had occurred at noon; no one had seen
his grandmother; a few shops were still open;
he went in, made inquiries, and got laughed
at for his pains. After wandering up and
down until one, he went home, convinced that,
in the agony of her remorse, his grandmother
had made away with herself. "She need not
have been afraid, I would have forgiven her,"
sadly thought Adrien. He had at first
doubted whether his knock at the door
would procure him admittance, but when,
in reply to a shrill inquiry, he had given his
name, it quickly opened. On seeing that he
was alone, Madame Moreau gave a peculiar
look and growl from beneath the shadow of
her peaked night-cap, and handing him a light,

an act of singular courtesy, said, "take that,"
almost gently.

Notwithstanding his sorrow, Adrien slept
that night—youth will sleep—but with a sad,
troubled slumber. Though the sun shone
brightly in the little room when he woke up,
he felt miserable. The unswept floor, the
fragment of his last hurried meal on the table,
the dusty mantel-shelf, the pot of réséda
drooping for want of water, everything, even
an old gown of his grandmother's thrown on a
chair, made him feel dispirited and low. He
rose and dressed hurriedly ; for breakfast he
cared not ; bread and dripping would do very
well. Scarcely was he attired when a knock
was heard at the door. "Tidings from her,"
thought Adrien, and he rushed to open.
Alas ! no ; it was only misanthropic Madame
Moreau, with an immense soup-plate full of
good beef-tea in her hand.

"Come, take it," said she, abruptly ; " you
want it, wandering all night ; those who did
the mischief were safe in bed ; maybe they
have good reasons to stay there," she added,
talking and nodding with deep sarcasm at the
door of Madame Mitron. "But next Mon-
day is rent day ; we shall see whether those

that drink and do not pay are to remain. Will you take this hot plate out of my hand, or am I to stay here all day?" she sharply added, turning round on Adrien. He was profuse in his acknowledgments, but without heeding them, she hobbled down-stairs, muttering her wonder that she had ever come up, and looking very surly, as though to apologize to herself for having committed this little act of kindness. As he drank his soup, Adrien thought how much his grandmother would have relished it, and then he wondered where she was that morning, and whether she had got any breakfast. This latter thought made him feel that he must resume his search without loss of an instant. In a few minutes he was ready, and proceeding hastily down-stairs. He had reached the third-floor when a hand, laid heavily on his shoulder, made him turn round ; he looked up, and saw Grand Jean.

"Adrien," said the tall Auvergnat, in a bashful, hesitating sort of manner, "I am not busy this morning ; I— I— can go with you, and help to look."

"You are very kind," replied Adrien ; and as he shook Jean's hand, he turned his head away; "very, especially after the insulting manner in which I spoke to you yesterday."

"Nonsense," said Jean, squeezing the lad's hand so hard that other tears besides those of emotion rushed to his eyes; "you never insulted me, child."

"Yes, indeed I did," remorsefully answered Adrien. "It was the tone, you know!"

"Well, never mind; I forgive you."

"Impossible!" resumed Adrien, somewhat nettled; "you do not know the badness there was in my heart against you. If it had not been for grandmother's sake, I would have knocked you down."

"Would you, indeed," said Jean, with a grave, good-humoured smile, and giving the lad a slap on the shoulder that made him stagger.

"Yes, I would," stoutly said Adrien, as soon as he had recovered his breath; "so pray," he mournfully added, "do not be kind; I cannot bear it."

"I tell you I bear no malice; and you are such an insignificant-looking little fellow, that people will never mind you if you go alone; so let us be off. '

Adrien bridled up, and wondered whether he

could in honour accept of assistance thus
offered. But Jean settled the matter by taking it for granted; and the lad, moreover,
secretly felt the force of his reasoning; so,
without further resistance on his part, they
sallied out. It was a hot, sultry day, and a long
and weary walk they had. They visited
barriers, and innumerable corps de gardes, or
station-houses, but no grandmother could be
found. "It is my fault," said Adrien, desperately; "I should have locked her up."
Jean with difficulty persuaded him he was
not to blame. After a search of several hours,
Jean began to lose all hope, but Adrien seemed
unwearied. They at length lit on a clue to
the object of their search in a remote corps de
garde. An old, half-witted peasant-woman,
unable to give a proper account of herself, had
been apprehended the preceding evening.

"Where is she?" cried Adrien, eagerly
looking round. "Oh! she was gone before
the magistrate, and was probably tried for
vagabondage by this."

"Oh! Jean!" exclaimed Adrien, "let us go
before they send her to prison."

He started off, and sped along the street
at a rate with which Jean could scarcely

keep up, and which made sober passengers
stare. At length the police-court was
reached; it was crowded; Adrien pushed
right and left desperately, but in vain, till
Grand Jean, with two or three vigorous
elbowings, had cleared the way for his
friend. Adrien paused not to utter thanks;
he sprang forward to the front of the court;
a rapid glance showed him that the bewildered old woman who sat at the bar
wringing her hands, and answering, with
perplexed look, the questions of the magistrate, was indeed his grandmother. Forgetting everything in his joy, he hastily
exclaimed with his own cheerful, confident
voice, "Do not be afraid, grandmother; I
am here; they wont hurt you."

The old woman uttered a low exclamation, whilst every look went round the
court in search of her protector, and lit at
length on the diminutive form of Adrien
with mingled amusement and surprise.

"Who is that child? What does he
want?" asked the magistrate.

"I am not a child, sir," said Adrien,
colouring, and raising himself on tiptoe, "I
am a working man. I earn six francs a

week.   I am come for my grandmother,
whom Madame Mitron lured away."

"Is this old woman your grandmother?"
said the magistrate, smiling.

"Yes, sir," answered Adrien, sighing.
"If she only took my advice, and not
Madame Mitron's, she would not be here.
I am sure," he continued, somewhat huskily,
"I do not ill-use her; I would scorn to
ill-use a woman, much less my own grandmother.   But then she does not like dripping nor onion soup, and we cannot afford
butter or fricot (stew)."

"Do not be hard upon me, Adrien,"
sobbed the old woman.

"No, grandmother, I will not, and I am
sure Monsieur le President looks too kind
to be hard upon you either.   Monsieur
will reflect that you are old, weak-minded,
and that Madame Mitron, who is very
cunning, takes you out to drink at your
expense.   You do not drink, grandmother,"
he added, anxious to save her from the
reproach of drunkenness, that most un-
womanly vice, so rare in France.

"And, Monsieur le President," here interposed Jean, laying his heavy hand on

Adrien's shoulder, "spare the old woman for the sake of the lad, as honest a one as ever breathed. If," he continued, heedless of Adrien's indignant looks, " if he does talk too much like a man, for one with such a beardless chin, why I say it is because he has the heart of a man."

The magistrate smiled. " You are discharged," said he to the old woman. "Believe me, abide by your grandson's advice, and shun Madame Mitron."

He rose, for this was the last case, the assembly dispersed, and in a few minutes the place was empty.

Adrien's grandmother looked very much humbled and cast down as they went home. This distressed him infinitely ; he did his best to cheer her, invented numberless excuses for her, and threw all the blame on luckless Madame Mitron.

" But where is Jean? " said he, suddenly breaking off, and looking round as they turned the corner of their own street. Jean had vanished, and though Adrien knew it not, it was some time since they had parted company. Although evening was drawing on, Madame Moreau did not occupy that

post on the door-step from which she surveyed and attacked the world. Adrien
peeped into the lodge as he took his key;
the lamp was as usual dimly burning, but
she who kept alive that sacred flame was
invisible.

"Grandmother," said Adrien, as they
went up the staircase, "you are hungry of
course; but," added he, looking at her
wistfully, "I can only give you onion soup."

"Anything, Adrien," sobbed the old woman; "dripping itself is too good for me."

"No, that it is not," said he, resolutely;
"and if," he added, raising his voice, "if
any one should look sideways at you for
what has passed, let that person expect to
settle it with me. And if," he continued,
louder still, and looking defiantly at Madame Mitron's door, for they had reached
their own landing, "if certain nameless
individuals, be they men or be they women," he loved the plural number for its
dignity, "should attempt to mislead you
again, let them understand that they have
been mentioned to the magistrate, and that
there are such things as commissaries of
police." Here Adrien paused, in order to

give Madame Mitron time to come forth and answer his challenge, but she remained within, fairly owning herself conquered.

When they entered their own little room, Adrien stopped short, and uttered an exclamation of surprise : the floor was swept, the place had been carefully dusted and set to rights, the réséda was itself again, the table was laid out, and the charcoal fire only needed the application of a lighted match.

" This is all Madame Moreau's doing," said Adrien, " and I," he remorsefully added, " I, who said so often she was a sour old thing ! Grandmother," he continued in his habitual and cheerful tone, " just light the fire, if you please. I will peel the onions."

In a few minutes the fire was kindled, the dripping was hot in the pan, and the onions on being cast in filled the room with their merry, hissing sound.

" Grandmother," exclaimed Adrien, with glee, " it will be, though made with dripping, the best soup you ever had. Not, mind you," he prudently added, " that butter may not be preferable for some tastes, but if one cannot afford it, what is the use of not making the best of what one has ? "

A knock at the door interrupted Adrien's discourse. " Come in," cried he, thinking it was Jean. It was not Jean; it was a waiter from a neighbouring cook-shop, who deposited a tray of covered dishes on the table.

" Monsieur Adrien ; paid for," said he, sententiously, and he left the room; whilst Adrien and his grandmother looked at one another in mute surprise.

" Ah ! " suddenly cried Adrien, " I see now why Jean left us. Grandmother, look ! here is a splendid stew of mutton and haricots ; you wished for one. And see this magnificent piece of veal ! Why there is enough for a week ! Oh, where is Jean ? "

He flew down-stairs, and searched on every one of the seven floors, but neither Jean nor Madame Moreau were to be found ; like the genii of an eastern tale, they vanished when their favours were conferred.

" Grandmother," said Adrien, as returning from his fruitless search he sat down with his old relative to their luxurious meal, " I

hope you will never go out again with Ma·
dame Mitron; but if you had not gone, we
should never have —"

"Had this good dinner," put in the old
lady, whose gourmandise was not quite subdued.

"No, grandmother," said he, gravely, "we
should never have known how much kindness
towards us there lay hidden in the hearts of
Madame Moreau and Grand Jean."

Three years have passed away: Adrien, cheerful, honest, industrious as ever, inhabits the
sunny old garret; but he has taken for his
grandmother the room formerly occupied by
Madame Mitron, who was disgracefully expelled
shortly after the events we have narrated.
Since this fortunate occurrence, his old relative
has given Adrien no further trouble; and, as
his earnings have greatly increased, they live,
as he says, "in luxurious style." Grand Jean
still dwells in the gloomy old house. He and
Adrien are great friends; he occasionally ban-
ters the youth, who has not grown much, on
his diminutive appearance; but Adrien, mindful of former kindness, and proud of his
dawning moustache, takes it all very good-
temperedly. Madame Moreau is as mis-

anthropic as ever; but, as Adrien says, " she is found out, and no one believes her now." This, however, excites great wrath in the old portress, who takes as much pride in her fancied scorn and hatred of mankind, as others are apt to take in their imaginary philanthropy and benevolence.

THE MYSTERIOUS LODGER.

WHO does not like mystery? The heart-
less, the cold, the unimaginative assuredly.
All poetical natures love it and live in it.
Without mystery they exist not. Life is dull,
commonplace, and cold, unless they have it.
Give it to them, therefore, by all means. Let
the Radcliffian cup of romance— but we will
not anticipate.

Monsieur Hyacinthe was a widower of middle
age and retired habits. He was pale, thin,
and bald, but these unromantic peculiarities in
his personal appearance did not prevent him
from being a passionate lover of romance and
mystery. Indeed it is a vulgar and sad mistake to suppose that only youth and beauty
love romance and mystery. Youth and
beauty have a great many other matters and
objects to engross their attention. It often
happens, too, that they are cool, calculating,

and sometimes actually inclined to worldliness.

Monsieur Hyacinthe was timid and somewhat cautious. The world was so mysterious,
the people in it were so full of mysteries, that
really one could not be too careful. Thus
Monsieur Hyacinthe had got to be on his
guard with every one, from his important and
stately landlord, Monsieur Moreau, down to
his sharp-tempered portress, Madame Latour.

Owing to this peculiarity in his temper,
Monsieur Hyacinthe resided alone in a small
apartment on the third-floor of a quiet house
in a lonely street. He kept no servant; the
danger of living alone was not equal to the
peril of having a perpetual spy and watch by
his side, or, to use Monsieur Hyacinthe's own
words, "of cherishing a foe in his bosom."
But if Monsieur Hyacinthe had no servant he
had a servant's room, which he prudently
under-let furnished when he could possibly
secure a lodger, which was but seldom, owing,
perhaps, to the gins and traps, in the way of
preliminary conditions, with which he cautiously intrenched his premises. This room was
in its usual state of vacancy, and Monsieur
Hyacinthe, after perplexing his mind to dis-

cover for what peculiar motive his room did
not let when other rooms let all around him,
had come to the conclusion that there was a
fatality in it.

"There is a fatality in it," he muttered,
drawing on his night-cap ; and settling himself
comfortably by the fireside, he opened his
newspaper in order to read the detailed account of the last murder : like many timid individuals, Monsieur Hyacinthe delighted in
the sad and the horrible.

Monsieur Hyacinthe had not read a line,
when he was disturbed by a ring at the door.
He laid down his paper, and with the coolness
which a constant habit of such thoughts
rendered natural, he said meditatively :

"Thieves! Of course I shall not open. It
is too early for burglars."

The ring was impatiently repeated.

"A visitor, perhaps!" pursued Monsieur
Hyacinthe. "Let him stay out—it is too late
to receive visits."

A third time the ring was heard.

Monsieur Hyacinthe's heart turned cold.
Such a ring at nine at night must be thieves,
visitors, or fire. No sooner did the last fearful suggestion offer itself to his mind than,

forgetful of his night-cap or every prudential consideration, Monsieur Hyacinthe precipitately rushed to the door, which he flung open.

A pale, slender, fair-haired young man about twenty, but whose manners were remarkably cool and self possessed, was standing on the landing. He was showily attired, and smelt very strongly of Eau de Cologne; the thumb of his left hand was placed in his corresponding waistcoat pocket; in his other hand he held a small and flexible badine.

"Well, sir," said he, frowning on Monsieur Hyacinthe, as much as his very smooth forehead and eyebrows would allow him to frown, "do you know that I have rung five times at your door?"

"I protest, sir," stammered forth Monsieur Hyacinthe, "I only heard three rings."

"Then, sir," observed the stranger, sternly eyeing him from head to foot, "then, sir, it was extremely, exceedingly impertinent in you not to open sooner. You have a room to let —show it to me."

But Monsieur Hyacinthe, who disliked this authoritative tone, promptly replied that it was too late to see the room. "It is not the

legal hour, sir," he said, with some dignity;
"the legal hour is from noon till sunset."

The stranger smoothed his chin, smiled, and
replied blandly:

"And so, sir, you actually think that a
gentleman will grope up three pair of stairs,
ring at doors, and walk down again, balked of
his will, because you please that it should be
so. Sir, why is there a bill up? I insist on
seeing the room."

Monsieur Hyacinthe protested, but the
stranger was peremptory; and as it was one
of his, Monsieur Hyacinthe's, maxims, that a
wise man ought to submit to anything in
order to avoid a present risk, he yielded at
length, though not without calling on every
one to witness that he was no longer a free
agent. As the stranger was the only person
who could hear this protest, it was useless;
but Monsieur Hyacinthe's conscience was
satisfied—he had done everything which a
brave and peaceable man could do, and he
proceeded to show the furnished room to the
stranger, now fully warned of his illegal conduct. The young man cast a careless look
around him, observed that the room suited

him, and throwing two gold pieces on the
table, bade Monsieur Hyacinthe pay himself
for the first month's rent, and keep the
change until another month was up.

" Sir," said Monsieur Hyacinthe, "you
have not heard my conditions. I am a
quiet man, sir; this room is near my rooms;
I like to be quiet. I allow no noise, sir, no
loud talking, never any music or singing on
any account. And I am particular, sir, very
particular. I feel convinced this room would
never suit you."

" I like it," said the stranger, "and I like
you."

Monsieur Hyacinthe nevertheless was going
to declare that, though his visitor liked him,
the room was not suited to him, and would
not do at all, when the young man, not giving
him time to remonstrate, proceeded to inform
him that he could apply to Madame Sébillard, number three, the next street, his present
landlady and abode, for references; but that,
as he hated hypocrisy, he would give him
his character himself; and in order to do this
with due comfort, he composedly sat down on
the bed.

" My name," he began, " is Henri Renaudin.

Is it my real name? That is of no consequence. My father is rich : I might live
in his hotel if I liked ; but there is a step-
mother in the way, and I wish to be free.
Still you will say—Why come to a poor
place like this ? I have private reasons for
doing so ; but to satisfy you, we will say a
whim brought me hither, or rather let it be
the wish of studying human nature in all its
infinite variety ;" and as though pleased
with this euphonious sentence, M. Renaudin
repeated it several times in a complacent
tone.

M. Hyacinthe here wanted to slip in a
remark ; but the other was too quick for
him. "I know what you are going to say
—Does my father allow me much? No ;
but I make him pay the same tailor's bills two
or three times over : I never pay my tailor
myself ; it is really too shabby," added M.
Renaudin, with profound contempt for the
meanness of such an act. "You need not
speak," he continued, seeing that M.
Hyacinthe was opening his mouth ; " I
know what you are going to say—How do
I get money ? The easiest thing in the
world : I have already spent three fortunes,

of which I never touched a sou. My mother's fortune was the first. Oh, no! now I think of it, it was my cousin's five hundred thousand francs that went first. Ah! they are all gone. Then came my mother's property—gone too: and my old uncle's fortune is going now. He is still alive, but he has made a will in my favour, so that I live on my future expectations. You seem astonished; it is very easy: I can put you in the way: borrow money at the rate of two or three hundred per cent., spend it, give parties, and so forth; you will find that a moderate fortune does not last much more than a year. But you look economical: well, then, let us say eighteen months, if you wish to see old Isaac."

"Thank you, sir," precipitately interrupted M. Hyacinthe: "you were speaking about your character?"

"You are welcome to it. In the first place, I am a dreadful gambler and a fearful spend-thrift. I delight in throwing money out of the windows, and seeing the people rush and fight for it. Does this window look out on the street? No: ah, sorry for it. Never mind, we shall find an opportunity. I see

you are greatly shocked; can't help it, my
dear sir—family failing—my mother was a
charming woman, but very extravagant, yet
greatly admired by the other sex; and, to say
the truth, I believe that I have also inherited
this peculiarity—that is to say, reversed; but
I hate vanity, so we will drop the subject.
Well, I think you have my character correctly
now. Stop, I was forgetting one very
remarkable peculiarity: I am dreadfully
violent, a famous duellist, and when excited,
would no more mind throwing you out of the
window than I would the smoking of a cigar;"
and as an apt illustration of this happy
comparison, M. Renaudin drew a cigar from
his cigar-case, and lighting it from the candle
held by M. Hyacinthe, began smoking it with
great composure.

" Sir," ejaculated the alarmed M. Hyacinthe,
endeavouring to smile, "this is only some
pleasant joke of yours. Remember the window
is very high; you would not have the heart
to throw a poor man from a third-floor?"

But M. Renaudin said he had the heart to
do anything; should feel extremely sorry
when it was all over, but could not help it;
had therefore thought it best to mention

this weakness, as it would be more pleasant to both parties if nothing of the kind occurred. "And now," he added, "that everything is explained, I think that, as I feel rather sleepy, you may leave me."

"I cannot allow that," uneasily exclaimed Monsieur Hyacinthe; "I must give notice to the police."

"I scorn the police," answered Renaudin, with deep contempt.

"Sir," indignantly exclaimed Monsieur Hyacinthe, who was gradually edging towards the door, "you fail in the respect due to the constituted authorities: your language is very illegal."

"I delight in everything illegal," was Renaudin's profane reply.

"Then, sir," resolutely observed Monsieur Hyacinthe, now on the landing, "I shall alarm the house."

"Do," answered Monsieur Renaudin; "there will be noise, fighting, smashing of window-panes, &c.,—things in which I rejoice— another trait in my character. But if you have a bone or two broken in the affray, do not say you received no warning."

This was uttered with such suavity of man-

ner, and the speaker had such a fair, meek
face, of which the most prominent features
were large eyes of a pale blue, a fat nose, and
a retreating chin, that he did not seem the
most likely individual to carry his threat into
execution; but Monsieur Hyacinthe, who
knew what horrible mysteries often lay hid
under the fairest aspect, and who never trusted
to personal appearances when his safety was
at stake, submitted, though not without a protest, and ended by putting the two Napoleons
in his pocket, and leaving Monsieur Renaudin
master of the field of battle. Fear was not
his only reason for acting thus: being a considerate man, he did not like to disturb a
quiet house. Besides, he was not sorry to let
his room to an individual who could afford to
throw money out of the window; for though
it is very well to discountenance extravagant
people, every one knows that it is profitable
to deal with them in the long run. There
might be, too, a vague mysterious pleasure for
Monsieur Hyacinthe in having this mysterious
individual under the same roof with himself;
a pleasure the more exquisite, that his
tenant's room adjoined that in which he slept,
and that when he, Monsieur Hyacinthe, had

retired to bed, he could distinctly hear Monsieur Renaudin sneeze three times. Strange thoughts came to Monsieur Hyacinthe,—was this sneezing a signal, who knew, who could tell? Dreams of Renaudin breaking open his door, and approaching his bed-side with a scowl, soothed Monsieur Hyacinthe's slumbers that night.

Early the next morning the mysterious lodger went out. As soon as he was down the staircase, Monsieur Hyacinthe, who had a double key, entered his room, and with a sigh of relief found that Monsieur Renaudin had carried away nothing; which was the less surprising that, save an old candlestick and a pair of snuffers, there was nothing portable in the room.

This important fact being ascertained, Monsieur Hyacinthe hastened to call on Madame Sébillard.

He found a busy, talkative lady, whose thoughts did not seem to go beyond the concerns of the furnished house of which she called herself mistress. At first she completely misunderstood his purpose, and insisted on letting him her first-floor for the moderate sum of three hundred francs a month. "A bargain, I assure you," she said, "a dead bargain."

"Madame, you do not understand—"

"Oh, yes I do—you want that little back room with the chintz sofa. Well, then, you shall have it. I had promised it to the English lord; but you shall have it."

"Madame, you do not understand me," austerely resumed Monsieur Hyacinthe; "I came at this early hour to inquire into the character of a mysterious individual, who left you under strange and sudden circumstances yesterday evening. He called himself to me Renaudin; his real name you perhaps know."

Madame Sébillard's busy face took a touch of melancholy.

"It was a great pity," she said, "but what could I do? I liked him very much, the dearest, gentlest, meekest lamb I ever had, but what could I do? I put it to you, sir; if I did not take Renaudin's room I could not let my second-floor. He bore the dismissal with angelic sweetness, quite entered into my feelings, and went to you, I suppose."

"Madame, there is something in all this," suspiciously said Monsieur Hyacinthe. "You confess you dismissed this singular being from

your house.   What had he done? who, what
is he?"

"The sweetest-tempered lodger I ever had,
and the quietest," replied Madame Sébillard;
"I should have been delighted to keep him,
if I could have let my second-floor without
his room, but I could not.   It was sad, very.
As to what he does to earn a living, you had
better ask him—I always took him to be
an employé, or something of the sort."

This shallow attempt to impose on his
credulity, Monsieur Hyacinthe was going to
receive with an indignant remonstrance, when
the appearance of a yellow-haired English
family, in search of an apartment, made Madame Sébillard deaf and blind, or rather took
and transferred her senses from him to her
future lodgers.

Monsieur Hyacinthe withdrew, profoundly
disgusted with so much duplicity, and more
than ever convinced of the universal tendency
which every individual had to cheat and deceive him.   As he entered the house in which
he resided, meditating how all this would end,
Madame Latour, the portress, screamed shrilly
from her lodge:

"Monsieur Hyacinthe, will you please to

give me ten sous for that letter?—give it to
him, Minna,—and another time, Monsieur
Hyacinthe, I shall be obliged to you if you
will kindly tell me when you take in lodgers
at nine at night."

Madame Latour's niece, Minna, a stout, red-
haired girl, handed the letter to Monsieur
Hyacinthe, who hastily put it back on perceiving that it was directed to Monsieur
Renaudin.

"With anything belonging to that man,"
he said, solemnly, " I will have nothing to do.
There may be gunpowder in that letter, for all
I know."

" Gunpowder!" said Madame Latour, coming
forward, " smell it, Minna."

Minna did as she was bid, and declared the
letter was scented.

" Do not trust it!" ejaculated Monsieur
Hyacinthe, " and do not trust the man to whom
it is directed."

" I have a great mind to put a match to it,"
said Madame Latour, who had a Baconian turn
for experiments.

" The risk be on your own head,"
solemnly said Monsieur Hyacinthe, " but
mark my words, Madame Latour, distrust

that man—and mind your niece," he added,
darting a look at Minna, who heard him
with open mouth and eyes.

"Mind my niece!" echoed Madame
Latour.

"Ay, Madame Latour, mind her!" And
Monsieur Hyacinthe went up-stairs, leaving
Madame Latour much excited. Minna was
her niece, the daughter of her brother in
the country, confided to her especial care,
and Madame Latour was of opinion that
Minna required strict watching and sound
exhortation. Of the latter she now received
a reasonable dose, with the concluding and
irresistible argument of a slap on the face,
which Madame Latour held essential to
correct female discipline, and which, as a
dutiful and affectionate aunt, she would
not on any account have omitted.

Not satisfied with warning every one
against his lodger, Monsieur Hyacinthe
kept strict watch on his motions, so as to
leave him the scantiest opportunities of affect-
ing any mischief. But though his vigilance
was most persevering, he could discover
nothing reprehensible in the conduct of
Monsieur Renaudin, and for his opinion of

that singular individual he was obliged to rely a good deal on Monsieur Renaudin himself. This strange being went out early in the morning and came home late at night, just like the most commonplace biped. Occasionally, indeed, he hinted in a dark and gloomy tone at certain deeds in which he had been engaged during the day; but though Monsieur Hyacinthe's hair "stood on end to hear him," as he elegantly expressed it, this was all he could learn, and every one agreed that the information was exceedingly vague.

There was, however, a kind of fearful charm in Renaudin's conversation for the peaceful Hyacinthe; for though, of course, it was very shocking to hear his guest speak with unparalleled and revolting coldness of the innocent hearts he had broken through mere wantonness, and of the foes whom he had laid in mortal combat at his feet— without speaking of all the tailors' bills which he had never paid—every one knows that those are subjects of the most thrilling interest, and which for a long time formed the very staple of modern fiction.

No wonder, therefore, that Monsieur Hya-

cinthe, being fond of the dark and the dismal,
was fascinated by the gloomy discourse of
Renaudin. Nor was he the only person on
whom this mysterious individual exercised
an influence. Every one in the house, from
Monsieur Moreau the landlord, who lived
on the first-floor, to Madame Latour in her
lodge, and the little tailor in his garret,
declared there was something incomprehen-
sible about that man.

Monsieur Moreau, who, having once been
a deputy, and voted against the freedom of
the press, thought himself a marked man,
asserted that it would be prudent to turn
him out of the house at once, as he was
probably the spy of a gang of thieves or
conspirators, both of which characters were
in his opinion identical; Madame Latour
called him a libertine and mauvais sujet,
and strictly forbade her niece Minna to
cast even a look upon him; the old tailor
gave a very diffuse opinion, in which there
was something about the degeneracy of
human nature, and the cut of Monsieur
Renaudin's coat, which was not, it seems,
at all orthodox. Monsieur Hyacinthe, who
knew most on the subject, said least;

"for," as he sententiously observed, "walls had ears." Occasionally, however, he ventured to observe that there was something fatal about his lodger's look—that he was, like Napoleon, a child of destiny, &c.—with which observations every one agreed, as being remarkably applicable to Monsieur Renaudin.

But such, however, was the exemplary conduct of this strange individual, so regularly did he pay his rent, and so nearly did he, upon the whole, behave like other people, that every one began to think him a commonplace fellow, and some persons went so far as to complain that they had been taken in. But events showed that their murmurs had been premature, and Renaudin soon let them see what he could do.

Madame Latour rose one morning, unwarned by presentiments of evil against the approaching calamity. She called Minna, who slept in the same room, and on not hearing Minna answer she thought nothing, save that Minna was oversleeping herself. She took a jug of cold water, which she held a sovereign remedy against sleepiness, opened the curtains, and prepared to let a few warning drops fall on Minna's fair forehead; but, amazement! the bed was empty and cold,—Minna was flown.

There could be no doubt about it. The young girl's clothes and little valuables were gone, as well as her person. Madame Latour's carefully-guarded and admonished niece had run away. But with whom? Who could have thus fascinated her? Some one in the house, for Minna never went out. Was it Monsieur Moreau? Monsieur Hyacinthe, or the old tailor? Impossible! A flash of light crossed Madame Latour's mind,—it was Renaudin!

True, proof was wanting, but was tame, commonplace proof ever so potent as suspicion? Madame Latour's suspicion proved to be a magnifying-glass of first-rate power, for she alarmed the house, called landlord and lodgers together, and vowed to be revenged on the artful Renaudin, should he presume to show his face again in the house, which every one agreed to be extremely unlikely.

But Renaudin showed them that he was capable of anything, for he came home at his usual hour. Madame Latour began the attack by asking him politely—and her politeness, being very uncommon, always foreboded some deep insult — what he had done with her niece, Minna?

" Ay, sir," she continued, still sweet and smiling, " I should like to know — just out of curiosity—what you have done with her."

Monsieur Renaudin must have been a consummate actor, for his face expressed surprise apparently so unfeigned, that Monsieur Hyacinthe, who was listening and looking over the banisters, was almost staggered in his belief of Renaudin's guilt.

" What I have done with your niece," at length said the young man, " why, truly, nothing, Madame."

" I suppose, sir," sharply said Madame Latour, " I suppose, sir, you think I am blind, and that I did not notice the looks, sir, —mind, the looks my niece cast upon you ? "

Monsieur Renaudin smiled and stroked his chin.

" I confess you have me there," he said, blandly ; " why yes, she *did* look at me. She *did*, and I will not deny but she may have felt much, but I gave her no encouragement. On my honour, I did not."

"Sir, what do you mean?" fiercely asked Madame Latour. "Look at you! my niece look at you, a girl reared by me! Say that you stared at her, sir, in a shameful, shameless way, but do not presume to assert that she cast a glance at you."

This sudden and extraordinary contradiction struck Renaudin dumb. He stared at Madame Latour as if he thought that lady mad, and until she asked him what he meant by it, without giving him time to reply, she overwhelmed him with abuse. It was in vain that he opened his lips to answer her invectives by a word of self-defence; for when she at length paused, out of breath, Monsieur Hyacinthe, bending over the banisters, said meekly:

"Well, I do think, sir, that you ought to give up this young girl. I do think you ought."

"I think so too," said Monsieur Moreau, appearing at the head of the staircase, "I am the landlord of this house, and it is my duty to insist on the deluded Minna being given up to her afflicted aunt."

"And I say it is a shame Monsieur should talk as he has talked of a poor girl, who has given up everything for his sake," said the little tailor, who was sitting in the lodge.

" I protest against the disappearance of this little red-haired girl being laid at my door," indignantly exclaimed Renaudin. " It is a slander on my good taste to hint at it. A slander which I shall resent," he added, looking around him with a fierceness which produced immediate, but brief, silence; for Madame Latour, being now exhausted, became hysterical, and declared that her darling Minna being gone, she had nothing to live for; she partly revived, however, when her friends bade her rouse herself for the sake of her lodgers; and she even exerted herself so much as to promise Monsieur Renaudin, who was now going up to his room, that she would soon be revenged upon him.

" Go up, sir," she said, loftily, " go up. You shall suffer for this yet."

And faithfully, indeed, did she keep her word. During a whole week her foe could neither leave nor enter the house without hearing himself reproached by Madame Latour with the abduction of her niece. But hatred has quick instincts; and the portress soon perceived that the graceless Renaudin was rather flattered at being thus reminded of the impression he had produced on the too-susceptible heart of the fair Minna: she accordingly sought for a surer method of inflicting a wound, and soon found a very effectual one, which she practised thrice with great success. This was to sleep so soundly at night, that she never heard her enemy's knock at the door, and that, consequently, Monsieur Renaudin had to spend the night in the open air, which, as the portress managed to be particularly drowsy in rainy weather, was not always very pleasant. Of course when he came in in the morning, Monsieur Renaudin raved at Madame Latour in an awful manner, and uttered such fearful threats of vengeance, that the alarmed Monsieur Hyacinthe assured her the whole affair would end in something dreadful. But the portress was a dauntless woman; she continued to brave the anger of her foe in the most fearless manner, and seemingly without suffering in consequence.

Punishment, indeed, seemed in this case to fall on the head of the guilty individual; for such was the persecution Monsieur Renaudin sustained on the subject of Minna, that the unhappy gentleman declared, in a tone of despair, he would leave the house unless it ceased. From morning till night, indeed, he heard of nothing but Minna. The female lodgers looked upon him with evident horror; the men remonstrated with him; and even the timid Monsieur Hyacinthe used the most persuavive arguments in order to induce him to give up Minna.

" Sir !" exclaimed Monsieur Renaudin, rolling his blue eyes in a portentous manner, " if I hear the name of Minna again, I shall do something desperate !"

As it did not escape Monsieur Hyacinthe that his lodger, whilst speaking thus, grasped a small pocket-pistol which was lying on the table, he hastened to retreat ; but when he had left the room, he said in a loud tone, though perhaps not quite loud enough to be heard, " hard-hearted wretch !"

But the circumstance of the pistol, which he had never seen before, nevertheless dwelt in his mind. What did his lodger want it for ? A duel or a suicide ? Monsieur Hyacinthe inclined rather towards the latter supposition. It seemed exceedingly likely that something fatal had befallen the unhappy Minna, and in such a case it was only natural that the guilty

Renaudin's mind should be burdened with remorse; and every one knows that, in such dark and mysterious characters, remorse leads to the most dreadful extremities. The more he thought on the subject, the more Monsieur Hyacinthe became convinced that it was his lodger's intention to commit some rash act; and remembering, with the most disinterested humanity, that he owed him nearly two month's rent, he resolved to save him in spite of himself. He immediately communicated his suspicions to the portress and Monsieur Moreau, who both appeared much startled on hearing of the pistol. The landlord especially seemed thrown into an unusual state of agitation. He treated the idea of a suicide with mysterious contempt, and darkly asked Monsieur Hyacinthe if he had never heard of such things as political assassination, and pistol-shots being fired at marked men? After which he made some unintelligible allusion to a warning letter, but ended by declaring that the pistol should be secured by all means; and that, in order to prevent him from committing mischief, Renaudin should be locked up in his room. But who was to beard the lion in his den? The portress and Monsieur Moreau agreed that

Monsieur Hyacinthe was the most fit person
to be intrusted with such a task. This worthy
individual, however, who entertained a most
considerate regard for his personal safety,
declared it would be as much as his life was
worth to undertake such an office, as he knew
Renaudin would fight like a tiger; but he
hinted something about Monsieur Moreau's
great moral courage, and Madame Latour being
safe on account of her sex; upon which the
landlord eyed him askance, muttering something about hidden accomplices, whilst the
portress sharply asked "if Monsieur Hyacinthe
wanted to get rid of her that way?" It was at
length agreed that the deed should be effected
by cunning. At dead of night, therefore, when
every one in the house was safely in bed and
fast asleep, Madame Latour raised up an alarm
of fire in most unearthly accents. The lodgers,
being all warned, took no notice of the fact,
with the exception of the luckless Renaudin,
who flew out of his room, and rushed down-
stairs as pale and breathless as though it would
not have been as sure a method of committing
suicide to remain in bed whilst the house was
on fire as any other which he might adopt.
Monsieur Hyacinthe, who was lying in ambush

on the landing, immediately darted into the room, pounced upon the pistol, which was still lying on the table, caught up a box of razors, and hurried off with his spoil to his own apartment. On discovering that the alarm was a false one, Monsieur Renaudin, who only saw in this another method taken by his enemy the portress to annoy him, gave her a ferocious look, and walked up to his room. His ill-humour was too great to enable him to perceive his loss, and it lucklessly made him neglect to lock his door.

But the next morning Monsieur Renaudin missed his razors, then his pistol, and ended by discovering that he was locked up. His cries soon brought Monsieur Hyacinthe to his door. The worthy gentleman then explained to his lodger through the key-hole that he was to remain a prisoner until he could prove that he no longer entertained hostile designs against his own person, and might be trusted with a debt. He added, however, that if Monsieur Renaudin would solemnly promise not to throw himself into the Seine, nor to leap down from the towers of Notre Dame, nor to destroy himself in any manner whatsoever; and if he would pay down to him, Monsieur Hyacinthe, the two months' rent which he owed him, and another month's rent to which he was entitled, not having received warning, he would see what he could do in order to free him from his bondage in two or three days' time. These conditions were, however, indignantly rejected by Monsieur Renaudin, who vowed that he would have justice if there was law in the land, and appealed to the police for protection. But Monsieur Hyacinthe reminded him that, as he delighted in everything illegal, and scorned the police, he had no right to complain; and thus ended the conference.

After walking about his room for some time in a state of great indignation, Monsieur Renaudin gradually cooled down, and requested to speak to Monsieur Hyacinthe and Monsieur Moreau. When they were both on the landing, he again demanded an explanation of their conduct. Monsieur Hyacinthe replied by saying that a pistol had been found in his room, and by hinting something about the unhappy Minna.

"Minna again!" groaned the captive in a tone of despair; adding, with reckless calmness : " How long do you mean to keep me a prisoner, and when will you give me anything to eat ? "

Monsieur Hyacinthe pretended not to hear this last question ; and after a good deal of hesitation, Monsieur Moreau said something about feeding one's enemies, and promised to send up Monsieur Renaudin his breakfast. This meal, however, only consisted of a cup of cold coffee, with a very scanty supply of bread ; but such as it was, Monsieur Moreau took the precaution of not delivering it to the captive without previously exacting from him a solemn promise of not attempting to escape for the whole of that day. Monsieur Renaudin, who was hungry, would have promised anything, and readily complied with this condition ; the more so, as Monsieur Moreau artfully gave him to understand that he was going to get a déjeûner à la fourchette. When he saw the deceit which had been practised upon him, he gave vent to his irritated feelings in bitter and gloomy language " about blighted hopes, and people being driven to desperate deeds." Monsieur Hyacinthe, who was listening on the landing, shuddered as he remembered that the window was not fastened; but Renaudin was probably too much bent on vengeance to think of self-destruction, for he quietly ate his bread, drank his coffee, and when a few hours had passed away, asked if dinner was ever going to come up, or if they meant to starve him. In answer to this question, a dish of onion soup, with cold mutton and bread, soon made their appearance; but on beholding this sorry fare, Monsieur Renaudin became so indignant, that he threatened to break all the window-panes in his room. Monsieur Hyacinthe, alarmed by this menace, pacified him by a dubious promise of mending his bill of fare the next day. As he was meditating, however, on the best means of eluding this engagement, an event occurred which relieved him from his embarrassment.

News were received of Minna, who had now been gone more than a week. The father of the fugitive wrote to apologize for the conduct of his daughter, who, unable to bear a longer absence from home, had returned to the bosom of her family. Madame Latour was greatly incensed by this explanation of the guilty Minna's conduct; and though the innocence of Renaudin was now clearly proved, she threw the whole blame upon him. Every one, indeed, felt disappointed at this commonplace conclusion, and, like the portress, found fault with the luckless Renaudin. They had got into the habit of associating his name with that of Minna—no longer the unhappy; they had looked upon him with suspicion and horror; he had been for them that favourite theatrical character—the traitor of the melo-drama; and lo! he now turned out to be a false traitor! In short, Monsieur Renaudin was now despised for not having committed the act which had drawn down persecution upon him. Monsieur Hyacinthe himself, who, when pleading the cause of Minna, had termed his lodger "a hard-hearted wretch!" no sooner found him to be innocent, than he contemptuously called him "a mean and spiritless fellow!" Monsieur Moreau was the only individual who showed no disappointment or surprise. "He knew all along," he observed, "that Minna had nothing to do with Renaudin's presence in the house." And he dropped such mysterious hints on the subject, that every one shrewdly concluded there must be something in it. On being informed by Monsieur Hya-

cinthe of the turn the affair had taken, Monsieur Renaudin naturally enough expected to
be released from his captivity; but though his
landlord told him that he was free, it struck
Monsieur Renaudin that there was something
very peculiar in his manner as he did so.
Monsieur Hyacinthe's first act, when this explanation was over, was to request his lodger
to pay him the two months' rent, which
happened to be due that very same day.
Monsieur Renaudin threw him the money
with silent scorn; but without heeding this,
his landlord examined each piece of silver
with minute attention, counted and recounted
the sum, and at length, apparently satisfied
that it was right, put it into his pocket.
When this was over, he produced a small
packet of papers, which he laid on the table
before his lodger. Monsieur Renaudin saw
that the papers were the bills of different
tradesmen, concerning heavy debts contracted
towards them by a Monsieur de St Maur.
After eyeing them one by one with a bewildered look, he asked an explanation of
Monsieur Hyacinthe; but his landlord affected not to understand him. " Surely Monsieur needed no explanation ; tradespeople

had come to inquire whether Monsieur de St Maur lived in the house; and though Monsieur had changed his name, they gave such an accurate description of his person, that Madame Latour knew it must be he. He had nothing to do with the whole affair; and if the next time Monsieur went out he was apprehended by the gardes du commerce, he could not prevent it."

" Sir," said Monsieur Renaudin, with a sort of desperate calmness, " before we attempt to elucidate this new and mysterious affair, let me know whether I am to hear anything more about the unhappy Minna."

Monsieur Hyacinthe gravely replied that the Minna affair was over; on hearing which, his lodger thanked Heaven with great fervour —for he had felt it impossible to divest himself of secret misgivings on this point—and proceeded to inform him that he laboured under a mistake in supposing him to be Monsieur de St Maur. But Monsieur Hyacinthe only smiled incredulously. " It was no business of his, but Monsieur could not expect him to believe this." Such, however, seemed to be Monsieur Renaudin's intention ; but his efforts proved fruitless. Monsieur Hyacinthe remained

convinced that " Monsieur's real name was not
Renaudin, and must consequently be St Maur.
Monsieur had his private reasons for lodging
in such a poor place as this; Monsieur
thought it shabby to pay his tailor; evidently
Monsieur was the individual in question."

" Very well," returned the exasperated
Renaudin, " I suppose *I am* Monsieur de St
Maur. But granting this, what business is it
of yours ? " he fiercely added.

"Don't bully me, sir ! " loftily observed
Monsieur Hyacinthe, making a dignified retreat towards the door. " I am not one of
your unfortunate tradesmen to bear with it.
If you wish to leave this house, you can do so
at once."

" I protest against this," exclaimed a voice
from the landing ; " and I hope that if Monsieur has anything like decent feeling left, he
will wait for the arrival of the two police
officers for whom I am going to send, and
who cannot be long without making their appearance, and allow himself to be quietly
taken to prison."

" To prison !—police officers ! Well, what
have I done now ? " asked Renaudin, with a
gloomy smile. " Killed or murdered ? "

"Monsieur Hyacinthe," continued the voice on the landing, "I call you to witness that he has confessed his horrible intent in the plainest terms! No, sir, you have not done the deed, but your design against my life was not the less criminal. I consider my escape a miraculous one!"

At the conclusion of this speech, Monsieur Moreau, who was the speaker, ventured so far as to look into the room, though he prudently remained behind Monsieur Hyacinthe, whose person acted as an effectual shield for his own.

"Now what does *this* mean?" wildly exclaimed the unhappy Monsieur Renaudin.

"This means," continued Monsieur Moreau, "that Monsieur's real character and designs are now known; that there are such things as traitors among conspirators, and that people may receive letters by which they learn that they are going to be murdered; and though the name of the murdered may be concealed, Monsieur will easily understand that there is no difficulty in guessing at it."

The unhappy Monsieur Renaudin heard this speech in the silence of dismay; but when it was over—"So," he exclaimed, sinking down on a seat in a kind of solemn fury,

" so it seems no silly girl can run off, no madman squander his money, and no fool think
himself a murdered man, but I must be the
seducer, the spendthrift, and the assassin !
Really, gentlemen, I am greatly obliged to
you."

" Sir," dryly replied Monsieur Hyacinthe,
" I had your character from your own lips ;
and events have shown that you were, as you
boasted, remarkably sincere."

Monsieur Renaudin thrust his left hand
into the opening of his waistcoat, and assumed
the Napoleon attitude, in order to bid defiance
to his enemies with more effect ; but a bright
thought seemed to flash across his mind, and
he suddenly checked himself.

" Leave me," said he, in an authoritative
tone ; " and let me have pen, ink, and paper :
there is that on my mind which must be revealed.   Yes," he solemnly added, " all shall
be confessed.   But remember," he continued,
in a menacing tone, " to let no one even ap-
proach the door of this room, or linger on the
staircase, until half an hour at least has
elapsed."

Fear and curiosity induced Monsieur Moreau
and Monsieur Hyacinthe to comply with this

request; for the former was fully convinced that the alarmed Renaudin was going to sacrifice his friends to his safety, and reckoned on the names of a dozen accomplices at the very least; whilst Monsieur Hyacinthe gloomily congratulated himself on the tale of horror which his lodger was going to unfold. A lingering feeling of suspicion, however, induced them to remain on the first-floor landing until the half hour was over, when they impatiently hurried up-stairs. Renaudin's room door was partly open, and Monsieur Hyacinthe cautiously peeped in. A light was burning on the table, and a letter was lying near it; but Renaudin had vanished. The truth flashed across his mind; he rushed in, tore the letter open, and read its contents aloud:

"The manifold persecutions which I have endured in this house compel me to retire from the shelter of its inhospitable roof, as I feel convinced that designs against either my life or property are entertained by certain individuals who dwell beneath it. All I say to my persecutors is, that they may live to repent of their conduct."

"Monsieur Hyacinthe," exclaimed Monsieur Moreau, in a prophetic tone, "mark my words—I am a dead man ; " and he retired to his apartment with the heroic air of a man resigned to the prospect of being shot at the first opportunity.

But Monsieur Hyacinthe's personal fears were outweighed on this occasion by his curiosity, which was greatly excited by Renaudin's mysterious disappearance. Madame Latour's assertion, that the fugitive had effected his escape by going down a back staircase, and opening the street door whilst she was asleep in her lodge, he always treated with the contempt which such a commonplace explanation deserved. Indeed Monsieur Hyacinthe would have been rather sorry to find out the truth. As his late lodger owed him nothing, and had done him no real injury, he found it pleasant, upon the whole, to have been connected with such a fearful and desperate character. There was, as he poetically expressed it, " a horrid charm in it, and food for the imagination." Fate, however, seemed perversely bent on dispelling the romance and mystery with which he had invested Renaudin, and to show this luckless individual in the most commonplace aspect. In the first place, it was ascertained shortly after his disappearance that he was *not* Monsieur de St Maur; then, as though this was not bad enough, Monsieur Hyacinthe discovered, amongst the few articles which his lodger had left behind him, a small book, from which he learned that Monsieur Renaudin had 1500 francs in the savings' bank—a mean and paltry piece of economy, which made Monsieur Hyacinthe justly indignant, as affording another proof of the gross manner in which he had been taken in. He was still smarting under the mortification of this discovery, when a friend of his treacherous lodger came to claim, in his name, the pistol—which also turned out to be a mere counterfeit, as, whether loaded with powder or lead, it would not go off—the razors, and the book. Monsieur Hyacinthe delivered up the articles with a hope that this was the last time he should hear of their owner. Such, however, was not to be the case, for the very same day Madame Latour triumphantly asked him if he knew who Renaudin was? Monsieur Hyacinthe said " No," with the air of a man resigned to anything he may hear.

" I got it all out of his friend ! " exclaimed the portress, with evident exultation. " He is —a hairdresser ! "

Monsieur Hyacinthe was at first stunned by
this new blow : the splendid, the extravagant,
the terrible Renaudin a hairdresser ! But no : it
could not be : he would not believe it. But,
alas ! even his scepticism was obliged to yield
to the evidence of his senses ; for the hairdresser to whose establishment the redoubtable
Renaudin belonged, took a shop in a neighbouring street, so that longer doubt was impossible. There have been, however, such
things as romantic hairdressers ; but though
Monsieur Hyacinthe fancied for a time that Renaudin might belong to that class, this was a
short-lived illusion. The young man, according
to the universal testimony, led a most exemplary
life : instead of going to drink or dance at the
barrier, he spent his Sundays with his family,
occasionally indulging in the harmless amusement of taking out his sisters for a walk. On
learning these circumstances, Monsieur Hyacinthe bitterly declared that " he gave him up."
His only comfort under this trying dispensa-
tion was, that Renaudin afforded a living proof
of the tendency which made every individual
seek to cheat and deceive him.

There is no knowing how Monsieur Moreau
might have acted under the influence of the

dangerous neighbourhood in which he was now placed, if he had not discovered about this time that the anonymous letter which had caused him so much alarm was only a practical joke of one of his friends—a fact which he took in high dudgeon. As for Monsieur Renaudin, he seemed to bear very philosophically the degrading position to which he was reduced in the eyes of his former acquaintances. Perhaps he had learned, from personal experience, that though it is very fine and agreeable to be thought a desperate sort of character, it occasionally happens to be inconvenient, as there are simple people who will take you at your word, whatever ill qualities you may bestow on yourself. However that may be, it will perhaps be gratifying to the reader to state, that Renaudin continues to be the same exemplary character he always was ; he has forsworn all ambitious thoughts, and is satisfied with being considered one of the most prudent, economical, and gentle professors of his gentle craft.

AN EXCELLENT OPPORTUNITY.

THE Rue St Denis is a busy place in
Paris; for it is dirty, thronged, and wealthy.
We all know that those tall dingy houses
might be gilt if they chose, and that if they
remain gloomy and dull, it is because gloom
and dulness of aspect are business-like, and
have been so from time immemorial. Thus
on looking at those houses there arise in
the beholder's mind vague visions of vast
commerce; of bales of goods piled in lofty
rooms; of dusty ledgers and, account books,
a goodly library, and, above all, of busy
wrinkled men, who have grown bent and grey
in the noble art of making money.

The streets leading to the Rue St Denis
share in its privileges; they are dirty, gloomy,
and thoroughly business-like. In one of those
streets there stands a tall and ancient house,
not different in that respect from its neighbours, the lower portion of which is a large
mercer's shop. This establishment is held

to be one of the very best in the neighbourhood, and has for many years belonged to an
individual on whom we will bestow the name
of Ramin.

About ten years ago, Monsieur Ramin was
a jovial red-faced man of forty, who joked his
customers into purchasing his goods, flattered
the pretty grisettes outrageously, and now and
then gave them a Sunday treat at the barrier,
as the cheapest way of securing their custom.
Some people thought him a careless, good-
natured fellow, and wondered how, with
his off-hand ways, he contrived to make
money so fast, but those who knew him well
saw that he was one of those who "never
lost an opportunity." Others declared that
Monsieur Ramin's own definition of his
character was, that he was a "bon enfant,"
and that "it was all luck." He shrugged
his shoulders and laughed when people hinted
at his deep scheming in making, and his
skill in taking advantage of, excellent opportunities.

He was sitting in his gloomy parlour one
fine morning in spring, breakfasting from a
dark liquid honoured with the name of onion
soup, glancing at the newspaper, and keeping

a vigilant look on the shop through the open door, when his old servant Catherine suddenly observed :

" I suppose you know Monsieur Bonelle has come to live in the vacant apartment on the fourth floor ? "

" What ! " exclaimed Monsieur Ramin, in a loud key.

Catherine repeated her statement, to which her master listened in total silence.

" Well ! " he said at length, in his most careless tones, " what about the old fellow ? " And he once more resumed his triple occupation of reading, eating, and watching.

" Why," continued Catherine, " they say he is nearly dying, and that his housekeeper, Marguerite, vowed he could never get up-stairs alive. It took two men to carry him up ; and when he was at length quiet in bed, Marguerite went down to the porter's lodge and sobbed there a whole hour, saying, ' Her poor master had the gout, rheumatism, and a bad asthma ; that though he had been got up-stairs, he would never come down again alive ; that if she could only get him to confess his sins and make his will, she would not mind it so much ; but that when she spoke of the lawyer or the priest, he blasphemed at her like a heathen, and declared he would live to bury her and every body else." '

Monsieur Ramin heard Catherine with great attention, forgot to finish his soup, and remained for five minutes in profound rumination, without so much as perceiving two customers who had entered the shop, and were waiting to be served. When aroused, he was heard to exclaim :

" What an excellent opportunity ! "

Monsieur Bonelle had been Ramin's predecessor. The succession of the latter to the shop was a mystery. No one ever knew how it was that this young and poor assistant managed to replace his patron. Some said that he had detected Monsieur Bonelle in frauds which he threatened to expose, unless the business were given up to him as the price of his silence; others averred that, having drawn a prize in the lottery, he had resolved to set up a fierce opposition over the way, and that Monsieur Bonelle, having obtained a hint of his intentions, had thought it most prudent to accept the trifling sum his clerk offered, and avoid a ruinous competition. Some charitable souls—moved no doubt by Monsieur Bonelle's misfortune—endeavoured to console and pump him; but all they could get from him was the bitter exclamation, "To think I should have been duped by *him!*" For Ramin had the art, though then a mere youth, to pass himself off on his master as an innocent provincial lad. Those who sought an explanation from the new mercer were still more unsuccessful. "My good old master," he said in his jovial way, "felt in need of repose, and so I obligingly relieved him of all business and botheration."

Years passed away; Ramin prospered, and neither thought nor heard of his "good old master." The house, of which he tenanted the lower portion, was offered for sale: he had long coveted it, and had almost concluded an agreement with the actual owner, when Monsieur Bonelle unexpectedly stepped in at the eleventh hour, and by offering a trifle more secured the bargain. The rage and mortification of Monsieur Ramin were extreme. He could not understand how Bonelle, whom he had thought ruined, had scraped up so large a sum; his lease was out, and he now felt himself at the mercy of the man he had so much injured. But either Monsieur Bonelle was free from vindictive feelings, or those feelings did not blind him to the expediency of keeping a good tenant; for though he raised the rent, until Monsieur Ramin groaned inwardly, he did not refuse to renew the lease. They had met at that period; but never since.

"Well, Catherine," observed Monsieur Ramin to his old servant, on the following morning, "how is that good Monsieur Bonelle getting on?"

"I dare say you feel very uneasy about him," she replied, with a sneer.

Monsieur Ramin looked up and frowned.

"Catherine," said he, dryly, "you will have the goodness, in the first place, not to make impertinent remarks; in the second place, you will oblige me by going up-stairs to inquire after the health of Monsieur Bonelle, and say that I sent you."

Catherine grumbled, and obeyed. Her master was in the shop, when she returned in a few minutes, and delivered with evident satisfaction the following gracious message:

"Monsieur Bonelle desires his compliments

to you, and declines to state how he is; he will also thank you to attend to your own shop, and not to trouble yourself about his health."

"How does he look?" asked Monsieur Ramin, with perfect composure.

"I caught a glimpse of him, and he appears to me to be rapidly preparing for the good offices of the undertaker."

Monsieur Ramin smiled, rubbed his hands, and joked merrily with a dark-eyed grisette, who was cheapening some ribbon for her cap. That girl made an excellent bargain that day.

Towards dusk the mercer left the shop to the care of his attendant, and softly stole up to the fourth story. In answer to his gentle ring, a little old woman opened the door, and, giving him a rapid look, said briefly:

"Monsieur is inexorable; he won't see any doctor whatever."

She was going to shut the door in his face, when Ramin quickly interposed, under his breath, with "*I* am not a doctor."

She looked at him from head to foot.

"Are you a lawyer?"

"Nothing of the sort, my good lady."

"Well, then, are you a priest?"

"I may almost say, quite the reverse."

"Indeed you must go away, master sees no one."

Once more she would have shut the door; but Ramin prevented her.

"My good lady," said he, in his most insinuating tones, "it is true I am neither a lawyer, a doctor, nor a priest. I am an old friend, a very old friend of your excellent master; I have come to see good Monsieur Bonelle in his present affliction."

Marguerite did not answer, but allowed him to enter, and closed the door behind him. He was going to pass from the narrow and gloomy ante-chamber into an inner room— whence now proceeded a sound of loud coughing—when the old woman laid her hand on his arm, and raising herself on tiptoe to reach his ear, whispered:

"For Heaven's sake, sir, since you are his friend, do talk to him; do tell him to make his will, and hint something about a soul to be saved, and all that sort of thing: do, sir!"

Monsieur Ramin nodded and winked in a way that said "I will." He proved, however, his prudence by not speaking aloud ; for a voice from within sharply exclaimed :

" Marguerite, you are talking to some one. Marguerite, I will see neither doctor nor lawyer ; and if any meddling priest dare—"

" It is only an old friend, sir," interrupted Marguerite, opening the inner door.

Her master, on looking up, perceived the red face of Monsieur Ramin peeping over the old woman's shoulder, and irefully cried out ·

" How dare you bring that fellow here ? And you, sir, how dare you come ? "

" My good old friend, there are feelings," said Ramin, laying his hand on his heart,— " there are feelings," he repeated, " that cannot be subdued. One such feeling brought me here. The fact is, I am a good-natured, easy fellow, and I never bear malice. I never forget an old friend, but love to forget old differences when I find one party in affliction."

He drew a chair forward as he spoke, and composedly seated himself opposite to his late master.

Monsieur Bonelle was a thin old man, with a pale sharp face and keen features. At first

he eyed his visitor from the depths of his vast
arm-chair; but, as if not satisfied with this
distant view, he bent forward, and laying both
hands on his thin knees, he looked up into
Ramin's face with a fixed and piercing gaze.
He had not, however, the power of disconcert-
ing his guest.

"What did you come here for?" he at
length asked.

"Merely to have the extreme satisfaction of
seeing how you are, my good old friend. Nothing more."

"Well, look at me—and then go."

Nothing could be so discouraging : but this
was an excellent opportunity, and when Monsieur Ramin *had* an excellent opportunity in
view, his pertinacity was invincible. Being
now resolved to stay, it was not in Monsieur
Bonelle's power to banish him. At the same
time, he had tact enough to render his presence agreeable. He knew that his coarse
and boisterous wit had often delighted Monsieur Bonelle of old, and he now exerted himself so successfully as to betray the old man
two or three times into hearty laughter.

"Ramin," said he, at length, laying his thin
hand on the arm of his guest, and peering

with his keen glance into the mercer's purple
face, "you are a funny fellow, but I know
you; you cannot make me believe you have
called just to see how I am, and to entertain
me. Come, be candid for once; what do you
want?"

Ramin threw himself back in his chair, and
laughed blandly, as much as to say, " *Can* you
suspect me?"

" I have no shop now out of which you can
wheedle me," continued the old man ; " and
surely you are not such a fool as to come to me
for money."

" Money?" repeated the draper, as if his host
had mentioned something he never dreamt of.
" Oh, no!"

Ramin saw it would not do to broach the
subject he had really come about too abruptly,
now that suspicion seemed so wide awake—
the opportunity had not arrived.

" There is something up, Ramin, I know;
I see it in the twinkle of your eye: but you
can't deceive me again."

" Deceive *you?*" said the jolly schemer,
shaking his head reverentially. " Deceive a
man of your penetration and depth? Impossible! The bare supposition is flattery. My

dear friend," he continued, soothingly, "I did not dream of such a thing. The fact is, Bonelle, though they call me a jovial, careless, rattling dog, I have a conscience; and, somehow, I have never felt quite easy about the way in which I became your successor downstairs. It *was* rather sharp practice, I admit."

Bonelle seemed to relent.

"Now for it," said the opportunity-hunter to himself.—"By-the-by" (speaking aloud), "this house must be a great trouble to you in your present weak state? Two of your lodgers have lately gone away without paying—a great nuisance, especially to an invalid."

"I tell you I'm as sound as a colt."

"At all events, the whole concern must be a great bother to you. If I were you, I would sell the house."

"And if I were *you*," returned the landlord, dryly, "I would buy it—"

"Precisely," interrupted the tenant, eagerly.

"That is, if you could get it. Phoo! I knew you were after something. Will you give eighty thousand francs for it?" abruptly asked Monsieur Bonelle.

"Eighty thousand francs!" echoed Ramin.

"Do you take me for Louis Philippe or the Bank of France?"

"Then we'll say no more about it—are you not afraid of leaving your shop so long?"

Ramin returned to the charge, heedless of the hint to depart. "The fact is, my good old friend, ready money is not my strong point just now. But if you wish very much to be relieved of the concern, what say you to a life annuity? I could manage that."

Monsieur Bonelle gave a short, dry, church-yard cough, and looked as if his life were not worth an hour's purchase. "You think your-self immensely clever, I dare say," he said. "They have persuaded you that I am dying. Stuff! I shall bury you yet."

The mercer glanced at the thin, fragile frame, and exclaimed to himself, "Deluded old gentleman!" "My dear Bonelle," he continued, aloud, "I know well the strength of your admirable constitution; but allow me to observe that you neglect yourself too much. Now, suppose a good sensible doctor—"

"Will you pay him?" interrogated Bonelle, sharply.

"Most willingly," replied Ramin, with an eagerness that made the old man smile. "As to the annuity, since the subject annoys you, we will talk of it some other time."

"After you have heard the doctor's report," sneered Bonelle.

The mercer gave him a stealthy glance, which the old man's keen look immediately detected. Neither could repress a smile : these good souls understood one another perfectly, and Ramin saw that this was not the excellent opportunity he desired, and departed.

The next day Ramin sent a neighbouring medical man, and heard it was his opinion that if Bonelle held on for three months longer, it would be a miracle. Delightful news !

Several days elapsed, and although very anxious, Ramin assumed a careless air, and did not call upon his landlord, or take any notice of him. At the end of the week old Marguerite entered the shop to make a trifling purchase.

"And how are we getting on up-stairs?" negligently asked Monsieur Ramin.

"Worse and worse, my good sir," she sighed. "We have rheumatic pains, which

make us often use expressions the reverse of
Christian-like, and yet nothing can induce us
to see either the lawyer or the priest; the
gout is getting nearer to our stomach every
day, and still we go on talking about the
strength of our constitution. Oh, sir, if you
have any influence with us, do, pray do, tell
us how wicked it is to die without making
one's will or confessing one's sins."

"I shall go up this very evening," ambi-
guously replied Monsieur Ramin.

He kept his promise, and found Monsieur
Bonelle in bed, groaning with pain, and in
the worst of tempers.

"What poisoning doctor did you send?" he
asked, with an ireful glance; "I want no
doctor, I am not ill; I will not follow his
prescription; he forbade me to eat; I *will*
eat."

"He is a very clever man," said the visitor.
"He told me that never in the whole course
of his experience has he met with what he
called so much 'resisting power' as exists in
your frame. He asked me if you were not of
a long-lived race."

"That is as people may judge," replied
Monsieur Bonelle. "All I can say is, that

my grandfather died at ninety, and my father at eighty-six."

"The doctor owned that you had a wonderfully strong constitution."

"Who said I hadn't?" exclaimed the invalid, feebly.

"You may rely on it, you would preserve your health better if you had not the trouble of these vexatious lodgers. Have you thought about the life annuity?" said Ramin, as carelessly as he could, considering how near the matter was to his hopes and wishes.

"Why, I have scruples," returned Bonelle, coughing. "I do not wish to take you in. My longevity would be the ruin of you."

"To meet that difficulty," quickly replied the mercer, "we can reduce the interest."

"But I must have high interest," placidly returned Monsieur Bonelle.

Ramin, on hearing this, burst into a loud fit of laughter, called Monsieur Bonelle a sly old fox, gave him a poke in the ribs, which made the old man cough for five minutes, and then proposed that they should talk it over some other day. The mercer left Monsieur

Bonelle in the act of protesting that he felt as
strong as a man of forty.

Monsieur Ramin felt in no hurry to conclude the proposed agreement. "The later
one begins to pay, the better," he said, as he
descended the stairs.

Days passed on, and the negotiation made
no way. It struck the observant tradesman
that all was not right. Old Marguerite
several times refused to admit him, declaring
her master was asleep : there was something
mysterious and forbidding in her manner that
seemed to Monsieur Ramin very ominous.
At length a sudden thought occurred to
him : the housekeeper—wishing to become her
master's heir—had heard his scheme and opposed it. On the very day that he arrived at
this conclusion, he met a lawyer, with whom
he had formerly had some transactions, coming
down the staircase. The sight sent a chill
through the mercer's commercial heart, and a
presentiment—one of those presentiments that
seldom deceive—told him it was too late. He
had, however, the fortitude to abstain from
visiting Monsieur Bonelle until evening came ;
when he went up, resolved to see him in spite

of all Marguerite might urge. The door was half open, and the old housekeeper stood talking on the landing to a middle-aged man in a dark cassock.

"It is all over! The old witch has got the priests at him," thought Ramin, inwardly groaning at his own folly in allowing himself to be forestalled.

"You cannot see Monsieur to-night," sharply said Marguerite, as he attempted to pass her.

"Alas! is my excellent friend so very ill?" asked Ramin, in a mournful tone.

"Sir," eagerly said the clergyman, catching him by the button of his coat, "if you are indeed the friend of that unhappy man, do seek to bring him into a more suitable frame of mind. I have seen many dying men, but never so much obstinacy, never such infatuated belief in the duration of life."

"Then you think he really *is* dying?" asked Ramin; and, in spite of the melancholy accent he endeavoured to assume, there was something so peculiar in his tone, that the priest looked at him very fixedly as he slowly replied:

" Yes, sir, I think he is."

" Ah!" was all Monsieur Ramin said; and as the clergyman had now relaxed his hold of the button, Ramin passed in spite of the remonstrances of Marguerite, who rushed after the priest. He found Monsieur Bonelle still in bed, and in a towering rage.

" Oh! Ramin, my friend," he groaned, "never take a housekeeper, and never let her know you have any property. They are harpies, Ramin,—harpies! such a day as I have had; first, the lawyer, who comes to write down 'my last testamentary dis-positions,' as he calls them; then the priest, who gently hints that I am a dying man. Oh, what a day!"

" And *did* you make your will, my ex-cellent friend?" softly asked Monsieur Ramin, with a keen look.

"Make my will?" indignantly exclaimed the old man; "make my will? what do you mean, sir? do you mean to say I am dying?"

" Heaven forbid!" piously ejaculated Ramin.

" Then why do you ask me if I have been making my will?" angrily resumed the old man. He then began to be extremely abusive.

When money was in the way, Monsieur Ramin, though otherwise of a violent temper, had the meekness of a lamb. He bore the treatment of his host with the meekest patience, and having first locked the door so as to make sure that Marguerite would not interrupt them, he watched Monsieur Bonelle attentively, and satisfied himself that the excellent opportunity he had been ardently longing for had arrived. " He is going fast," he thought; "and unless I settle the agreement to-night, and get it drawn up and signed to-morrow, it will be too late."

" My dear friend," he at length said aloud, on perceiving that the old gentleman had fairly exhausted himself, and was lying panting on his back, "you are indeed a lamentable instance of the lengths to which the greedy lust of lucre will carry our poor human nature. It is really distressing to see Marguerite, a faithful, attached servant, suddenly converted into a tormenting harpy by the prospect of a legacy! Lawyers and priests flock around you like birds of prey, drawn hither by the scent of gold! Oh, the miseries of having delicate health combined with a sound constitution and large property!"

"Ramin," groaned the old man, looking inquiringly into his visitor's face, "you are again going to talk to me about that annuity—I know you are!"

"My excellent friend, it is merely to deliver you from a painful position."

"I am sure, Ramin, you think in your soul I am dying," whimpered Monsieur Bonelle.

"Absurd, my dear sir. Dying? I will prove to you that you have never been in better health. In the first place, you feel no pain."

"Excepting from rheumatism," groaned Monsieur Bonelle.

"Rheumatism! who ever died of rheumatism? and if that be all—"

"No, it is not all," interrupted the old man with great irritability; "what would you say to the gout getting higher and higher up every day?"

"The gout is rather disagreeable, but if there is nothing else—"

"Yes, there is something else," sharply said Monsieur Bonelle. "There is an asthma that will scarcely let me breathe, and a racking pain in my head that does not allow me a moment's ease. But if you think I am dying, Ramin, you are quite mistaken."

"No doubt, my dear friend, no doubt; but in the mean while, suppose we talk of this annuity. Shall we say one thousand francs a year?"

"What?" asked Bonelle, looking at him very fixedly.

"My dear friend, I mistook: I meant two thousand francs per annum," hurriedly rejoined Ramin.

Monsieur Bonelle closed his eyes, and appeared to fall into a gentle slumber. The mercer coughed; the sick man never moved.

"Monsieur Bonelle."

No reply.

"My excellent friend."

Utter silence.

"Are you asleep?"

A long pause.

"Well, then, what do you say to three thousand?"

Monsieur Bonelle opened his eyes.

"Ramin," said he, sententiously, "you are a fool; the house brings me in four thousand as it is."

This was quite false, and the mercer knew it; but he had his own reasons for wishing to seem to believe it true.

"Good Heavens!" said he, with an air of great innocence, "who could have thought it, and the lodgers constantly running away. Four thousand? Well, then, you shall have four thousand."

Monsieur Bonelle shut his eyes once more, and murmured "The mere rental— nonsense!" He then folded his hands on his breast, and appeared to compose himself to sleep.

"Oh, what a sharp man of business he is!" Ramin said, admiringly: but for once omnipotent flattery failed in its effect: "So acute!" continued he, with a stealthy glance at the old man, who remained perfectly unmoved. "I see you will insist upon making it the other five hundred francs."

Monsieur Ramin said this as if five thousand five hundred francs had already been mentioned, and was the very summit of

Monsieur Bonelle's ambition. But the ruse failed in its effect; the sick man never so much as stirred.

"But, my dear friend," urged Monsieur Ramin, in a tone of feeling remonstrance, "there is such a thing as being too sharp, too acute. How can you expect that I shall give you more when your constitution is so good, and you are to be such a long liver?"

"Yes, but I may be carried off one of those days," quietly observed the old man, evidently wishing to turn the chance of his own death to account.

"Indeed, and I hope so," muttered the mercer, who was getting very ill-tempered.

"You see," soothingly continued Bonelle, "you are so good a man of business, Ramin, that you will double the actual value of the house in no time. I am a quiet, easy person, indifferent to money; otherwise this house would now bring me in eight thousand at the very least."

"Eight thousand!" indignantly exclaimed the mercer. "Monsieur Bonelle, you have no conscience. Come now, my dear friend, do be reasonable. Six thousand francs a

year (I don't mind saying six) is really a
very handsome income for a man of your
quiet habits. Come, be reasonable." But
Monsieur Bonelle turned a deaf ear to
reason, and closed his eyes once more.
What between opening and shutting them
for the next quarter of an hour, he at
length induced Monsieur Ramin to offer
him seven thousand francs.

" Very well, Ramin, agreed," he quietly
said ; " you have made an unconscionable
bargain." To this succeeded a violent fit
of coughing.

As Ramin unlocked the door to leave,
he found old Marguerite, who had been
listening all the time, ready to assail him
with a torrent of whispered abuse for dup-
ing her " poor dear innocent old master
into such a bargain." The mercer bore it
all very patiently ; he could make allow-
ances for her excited feelings, and only
rubbed his hands and bade her a jovial
good evening.

The agreement was signed on the following day, to the indignation of old Marguerite, and the mutual satisfaction of the
parties concerned.

Every one admired the luck and shrewdness of Ramin, for the old man every day was reported worse; and it was clear to all that the first quarter of the annuity would never be paid. Marguerite, in her wrath, told the story as a grievance to every one : people listened, shook their heads, and pronounced Monsieur Ramin to be a very clever fellow.

A month elapsed. As Ramin was coming down one morning from the attics, where he had been giving notice to a poor widow who had failed in paying her rent, he heard a light step on the stairs. Presently a sprightly gentleman, in buoyant health and spirits, wearing the form of Monsieur Bonelle, appeared. Ramin stood aghast.

"Well, Ramin," gaily said the old man, "how are you getting on? Have you been tormenting the poor widow up-stairs? Why, man, we must live and let live!"

"Monsieur Bonelle," said the mercer, in a hollow tone, "may I ask where is your rheumatism?"

"Gone, my dear friend,—gone."

"And the gout that was creeping higher

and higher every day," exclaimed Monsieur Ramin, in a voice of anguish.

"It went lower and lower, till it disappeared altogether," composedly replied Bonelle.

" And your asthma—"

" The asthma remains, but asthmatic people are proverbially long-lived. It is, I have been told, the only complaint that Methuselah was troubled with." With this Bonelle opened his door, shut it, and disappeared.

Ramin was transfixed on the stairs ; petrified with intense disappointment, and a powerful sense of having been duped. When he was discovered, he stared vacantly, and raved about an excellent opportunity of taking his revenge.

The wonderful cure was the talk of the neighbourhood, whenever Monsieur Bonelle appeared in the streets, jauntily flourishing his cane. In the first frenzy of his despair, Ramin refused to pay ; he accused every one of having been in a plot to deceive him ; he turned off Catherine and expelled his porter ; he publicly accused the lawyer and priest of conspiracy ; brought an action against the doctor, and lost it. He had another brought against him for violently assaulting Marguerite, in which he was cast in heavy damages. Monsieur Bonelle did not trouble himself with useless remonstrances, but, when his annuity was refused, employed such good legal arguments, as the exasperated mercer could not possibly resist.

Ten years have elapsed, and MM. Ramin and Bonelle still live on. For a house which would have been dear at fifty thousand francs, the draper has already handed over seventy thousand.

The once red-faced, jovial Ramin is now a pale, haggard man, of sour temper and aspect. To add to his anguish, he sees the old man thrive on that money which it breaks his heart to give. Old Marguerite takes a malicious pleasure in giving him an exact account of their good cheer, and in asking him if he does not think Monsieur looks better and better every day. Of one part of this torment Ramin might get rid, by giving his old master notice to quit, and no longer having him in his house. But this he cannot do; he has a sacred fear that Bonelle would take some excellent opportunity of dying without his knowledge, and giving some other person an excellent opportunity of personating him, and receiving the money in his stead.

The last accounts of the victim of excellent opportunities represent him as being gradually worn down with disappointment. There seems every probability of his being the first to leave the world; for Bonelle is heartier than ever.

THE

EXPERIENCES OF SYLVIE DELMARE.

CHAPTER I.

It was the eve of New Year's Day. I sat alone in the dining-room, now cold and dark; the drawing-room door was slightly ajar; I could see my step-mother sitting by the fireside; she looked smiling and pleased; her two daughters stood talking and laughing together on the hearth-rug; the lamp was still unlit, but the fire burned with a bright cheerful glow: I turned away my glance with a saddened heart.

This was the last day of the year, the day of Saint Sylvester, my patron saint,—yet who had offered me the bouquet of choice flowers? who had embraced me tenderly, and wished that this my fête day might be gay and happy?—No one.

It had not always been so. I remembered the wonderful nosegay my poor father never failed to provide on this day for his little Sylvie;

the mystery with which he placed it in her
room, so that it might be the first object to
greet her sight when she woke; his apparent
surprise as to how it had come there; and
then the sudden smile, the embrace and fond
kiss, all came back;· but this was over now;
he had been dead a year and more. I was a
portionless orphan of sixteen, and the only
legacy my father—a retired officer whose pen-
sion died with him—had been able to be-
queath to a step-mother, good indeed, but cold.

They had loved in youth, but been compelled to part. She was united to a rich old
man; my father loved again and married—
my mother, who died young: I was their only
child. He had been a widower for several
years, when he met once more his early love;
she also was free, with two daughters and a
handsome fortune: they married. They were
happy, but the fervour of their youthful
attachment was over; my step-mother could
scarcely forgive her husband the love he had
felt for his first wife; I saw that she was
jealous of the past, and that it pained her to
look on me, because I was said to be my
mother's living image. Yet when my father
was on his death-bed she promised him, of her

own accord, to bring me up with her daughters, and treat me as her child. She was an honourable woman, and rigidly fulfilled this engagement. I shared the studies of Joséphine and Louise, I was dressed like them, I went out with them, and·partook of all their pleasures; but my step-mother was a woman; I was the daughter of her rival, and she could not love me.

My feelings for her were contradictory. I sometimes loved and sometimes disliked her. I resented her indifference or blessed her goodness by turns. I would have given anything to be loved by her; I had even made a few timid attempts; but disheartened at their failure, I at length kept aloof, and widened that line of separation which she had imperceptibly established betwixt us. Yet the knowledge of her coldness always grieved me, and it was this that saddened me as I sat in the dining-room, unmissed and undisturbed, on the eve of New Year's Day.

Ere long I heard the great drawing-room door open; then a servant came in and laid down something on the floor. Louise and Joséphine uttered exclamations of delight.

"Beautiful! lovely!" they both cried. I

heard the rustling of silk. I knew the New Year's presents were come, that mine was amongst the rest, but I would not look, nor even confess to myself that I cared to look.

"I am glad you like them, my darlings," said the gentle voice of my step-mother; "where is Sylvie?"

"Moping, of course," replied the charitable Louise.

"Of course!" echoed her no less charitable sister.

I was called, and came forth resolved not to be pleased; but my heart relented at once when I saw the three dresses of blue silk lying on the sofa. I took up mine, looked at it, and turned towards my step-mother with flushed cheeks and sparkling eyes. I felt glad and grateful; I longed to go up to her, to say something, to embrace her, but there was little encouragement in her cold tone as she said, "Sylvie, here is your New Year's Day present," none in her calm face; besides, she was absorbed in looking at her daughters, who were already trying on their dresses. I sighed and followed their example. When Louise and Joséphine had been sufficiently admired by their mother, and had placed themselves

at every possible distance for her to see how
they looked, she turned towards the corner
where I stood apart and unheeded.   She
looked at me, then at her daughters, then at
me again, and a change came over her placid
countenance.   I felt distressed, for I knew
what   was   passing   in   her   mind.   The
daughters of my step-mother were wholly unlike her; she was pretty still, fair and delicate ; they were dark, coarse-skinned girls,
with hair as crisp as that of mulattoes.   I certainly was not handsome, but nature had
given me a profusion of golden-coloured hair,
blue eyes, and the clear complexion of youth.
I know not under what maternal delusion my
step-mother laboured when she chose a light
blue as the colour for the three dresses ; certain it is the effect for her daughters was de-
plorable.   They, poor girls, saw nothing of this,
but she did, and as the colour happened to
become me very well, she suffered doubly.

I felt truly grieved.   I would have given up
all the dresses in the world for one kind
glance, for one word of affection.   I looked at
my step-mother wistfully ; I wished her to
understand what I felt; but my appealing
look met with no reply ; her countenance was

overcast, and her eye averted from me. My
pleasure vanished, the present gave me no joy;
for though I had not worn it more than a few
minutes, it had already been the cause of pain
to the giver. I left the apartment in silence,
and went up to my own room more sad than
ever. What a difference between this and my
father's presents! He had once given me a
little printed muslin dress not worth more
than a few francs, but I remembered the delight with which I tried it on, and got up on a
chair to see myself in my very diminutive mirror,
and thought how gracefully the skirt fell in
long and ample folds, and how charming and
becoming a dress it was altogether. But the
costly silk yielded me no such gratification; I
sat down, heedless of creasing it, and without
so much as giving one glance at the looking-
glass. My heart was very full; I thought of old
times; of my dead father; of my step-mother,
whom I could have loved so dearly if she
would only have allowed me; of my loneliness
in this world, where no one cared for me.
" Oh! that some one would only let me love a
great deal, and love me a little in return," I
exclaimed inwardly.

My look here fell on an object which had

escaped it until then : it was only a nosegay
of white flowers, standing in a vase on my
dressing-table, but it made my heart beat as I
drew near it, and when I bent to inhale the fragrance of the pale blossoms, the tears I had
striven to repress till then, fell fast.   I knew
it was the old servant Catherine who had
placed those flowers there.   She, who had
known me from a child, loved me ; she had not
forgotten that this was the fête day of her
little Sylvie.   I felt comforted, and almost
cheerful.   There is something in true kindli-
ness that opens the heart.   What could old
Catherine do for me ?   Nothing; her good-
will was about as useful to me as the flowers
she had placed in my room in my absence, yet
both gladdened me, gave me new feelings and
new hopes.   I paced my room with a quick
step, forming schemes for the future, and
building castles in the air.   " I will not stay
here to have my heart daily wounded," I
thought with rising pride ; " I will not stay to
be a burden to those by whom I am not
loved : I will write to my god-mother."

I looked at my god-mother's portrait as it
hung on the wall before me, in order to con-
firm myself in this resolve.   The face was

young, and, if not good-looking, at least good-
natured. But it had been drawn many years
back, and I knew that the respected original
had now attained a good old age. She lived
in a quiet little town twenty leagues off; I
had no remembrance of her, and, to my knowledge, she had never sought to see me. I
dutifully wrote to her on the first day of the
year, and on the eve of her fête day. She gave
me short answers and her blessing: to this
was our intercourse limited.

But I was young and romantic, and I had
always settled it in my mind that my god-
mother, a rich old maid, with no near relatives, was to be the good fairy of my destiny. Now was the moment to test her.
My New Year's Day letter was not yet written;
I framed it according to my present mood.

At the end of a week I received the desired
reply. My step-mother seemed a little surprised at my god-mother's invitation for an
indefinite period, but observing "that Mademoiselle Tournelle probably meant to adopt
me," she quietly gave her assent. When the
day fixed for my departure arrived, I perceived
that I felt more sad than joyful at the success
of my scheme. It seemed unfriendly to leave

the familiar place, the step-mother, who, with all her coldness, had been so very good; the two girls, who, though often unkind, had called me sister. My heart yearned towards them in spite of repelled affection and wounded pride; but they had no such feelings. Louise and Joséphine saw me depart with evident pleasure; their mother gave me a cold embrace, that checked the thanks for past kindness ready to fall from my lips, and when I entered the little car that was to convey me to the diligence in the neighbouring town, no one, save old Catherine, stood on the doorway to see me depart, and wish me a happy journey.

CHAPTER II.

Long before I had reached my destination,
I had comfortably settled it in my own mind
that my god-mother was an angelic old lady,
who would soon doat upon me, for whom I
should entertain great affection and respect,
and who would find in me the staff and comfort of her old age. That she was a most
noble-hearted, amiable person I could not
doubt, for she had been betrothed in youth to
a gentleman who died young, and for whose
sake she was still a spinster, at the age of
seventy.

It was late when I arrived. The house of
my god-mother stood on the outskirts of the
town; it was a quiet-looking place, with a
narrow strip of garden. The diligence
stopped; I alighted; my trunk was lowered
down on the pavement; the guard blew his
horn; the postillion cracked his whip, and
the lumbering vehicle clattered down the narrow street. I gave the bell a timid, hesitating

jerk; a heavy step was heard in the passage, then the door opened, and an enormously stout old servant, holding a light in her hand, appeared on the threshold.

" Mademoiselle Tournelle," I said in a low tone.

The servant eyed me from head to foot, held up the light to see my trunk, then slowly looked at me again   The night was cold, the wind blew keenly, I became impatient.

" Mademoiselle Tournelle," I said again.

" Do you think I am deaf?" was the gracious answer of the fat servant. She condescended, however, to let me enter, and even bent her majestic person for the purpose of lifting up my trunk. After the most desperate efforts, she succeeded in dragging it in, puffing very hard and eyeing me askance all the time. Out of breath with this painful exertion, she silently pointed to a door on her right: I entered. The room was low, small, and oppressively warm. A large wood fire burned on the hearth; I felt a thick carpet under my feet; a lamp, suspended from the ceiling, gave a narrow circle of faint, dim light, and left the rest of the room in comparative obscurity. A wide couch, old high-backed chairs, a mahogany press that reflected the fire-light in its broad polished pannels, met my rapid glance. I looked for my god-mother, but all I could see was a dark massive-looking arm-chair by the fireside, and an old cat asleep on the hearth-rug. I was wondering whether my god-mother would soon make her appearance, when I heard a husky cough, which seemed to proceed from the depths of the arm-chair, and something strongly re-sembling—in the dark—a large black bundle began to agitate itself in the same quarter. I came quickly forward. I felt I stood in the presence of my god-mother—I was a foolish little thing in those days; I know not why a mist came over my eyes, and I know not how, instead of merely taking my god-mother's extended hand, I found myself on my knees before her, crying over the hand I had seized as if my heart would break, and sobbing " Marraine, Marraine ! "

"Oh ! mon Dieu ! who is this ? Is she mad ? Help ! Marianne ! "—a bell was rung violently—"the young lady is ill ; pick her

up, and "—wheeling back her chair—
" mind you do not let her come near me."

There was no need to pick me up. I was
on my feet in an instant, crimson with surprise
and shame.

" Is it a fever ? " continued my god-mother,
still wheeling back her chair, until it had
reached the wall. " Is it contagious ? " A scent-
bottle was at her nose directly.

I stammered forth that I was quite well.

" Are you sure of it ? " said she, eyeing me
cautiously ; " quite sure that you do not feel
feverish ? Are you subject to fits, or was it
only a fall ? Are you hurt ? Oh ! you need
not show me. Marianne, see if the young
lady is hurt."

I shortly answered that I was given to no
fits, and had sustained no injury.

" Then bring us in the supper, Marianne, it
will do us good; and you, my dear child, sit
down opposite me on the other side of the
fire-place that I may see you." So speaking
my god-mother wheeled slowly back to her
former place, keeping her eye on me all the
time, and remaining at a prudent distance.
I took the seat she pointed out, and being

still astonished and confused, eyed her with a
bewildered glance.

I had thought Marianne stout, but, compared
to her mistress, she was a light and agile
maiden. Mademoiselle Tournelle was the
broadest lady I ever beheld; the horizontal
line predominated throughout her whole
person. I never saw anything so compact
as herself and the arm-chair together: she
fitted in the arm-chair, and the arm-chair
fitted to her with mathematical accuracy;
I thought of a plump oyster in its shell, and
wondered whether she ever got out of it.

After looking at me for some time, and
becoming convinced of my harmlessness, my
god-mother hoped in a husky voice that my
fall had not hurt me. I explained that it was
not exactly a fall had brought me at her feet.

"Oh!" she slowly said, "I thought it
was; you see at my age people have done
with kneeling, weeping, and sentiment:
things which only tend to disturb the diges
tion."

I murmured an apology.

"Never mind. So you were not comfortable
at home." I wished to explain, she would not

allow me—" No details, my dear child, they are
useless and distressing things : I can imagine.
Take off your cloak and bonnet ; here comes the
supper."

Marianne entered, bearing a covered dish,
from which a fricassée of hot rabbit sent forth
a most savoury odour.   My god-mother's little
black eyes sparkled, her lips moved and
moistened, she wheeled her chair to the table,
smoothed down the table-cloth, opened and
spread out her own immaculate napkin, and,
with her eyes on the dish, she softly rubbed
her fat white hands.   She did not seem in any
hurry : no, she waited for the happy moment
in a sort of placid beatitude, that bespoke the
serenity of her mind.

" So this is my god-mother ! " thought I,
watching her picking the choice bits out of the
dish, with all the candour of genuine selfishness and gourmandise.

" Do you like hot fricassée of rabbit, my
dear ?   You do.   I am so glad.   There is nothing more uncomfortable than want of sympathy.   I was to have married a gentleman, a
good man certainly, but with whom I could
never agree.   He detested my fricassée, and I

detested his pâté de foie : it ended by
carrying him off, as I had always pre-
dicted."

After supper, which lasted for an hour, my
god-mother, not seeming to think that I might
be fatigued and need rest, asked me to read her
to sleep with the newspaper : in two minutes
she was in a comfortable doze, which lasted
half an hour. At the end of that time she
woke up quite refreshed, and rang the bell.
Marianne entered, carrying a tray covered with
delicacies, which she placed on a convenient
little table at my god-mother's elbow ; she
next brought forward a very comfortable high-
backed chair, then a soft cushion for the feet,
and placing both opposite the fire, composedly
seated herself near her mistress, with whom she
began to discuss the menu of the next day's
dinner.

"Potage au riz, Marianne, it is long since we
had any."

"I have no objection to the potage ; but you
must have côtelettes au basilic for the second
course."

"With a poularde à la bourgeoise," placidly
suggested my god-mother.

" No, indeed," snappishly said the cook,
" you shall have ducks en hochepot, and be glad
to get them too."

My god-mother yielded the point with a
sigh: she evidently requested the poularde.
The third course was extremely stormy: the
mistress insisted on partridges, the cook declared she should be satisfied with a poulet à
la reine. Overpowered with fatigue, I fell
asleep as they renewed the quarrel over the
dessert.

I remained with my god-mother a whole
year, during which I was oppressed with comfort, and loaded with good things. There was
not a genuine angle in the whole house.
Everything was softened down, cushioned, and
rounded off, as if for the use of the most fragile
being. The beds of painful softness were
shrouded in by drowsy-looking curtains; the
doors had thick coats of wadding on, and flew
open before the slightest touch; there were
thick blinds to keep out the light, and high
screens to keep off the wind; the chairs were
vast and deep, the cushions soft and easy. But
what was this to our perpetual feeding? Breakfast at eight, déjeûner à la fourchette at eleven,
goûter at two, dinner at six, and supper at nine.

At the end of a week I declared I could not possibly partake of more than three meals a day, and sank for ever in the esteem of my god-mother and her cook Marianne.

For all this she was one of the most good-natured of selfish gourmands, quite ready to do a kindness, if she were only put in the way. This indeed was an indispensable condition. I do not think she doted on me, and my romantic fancies of being the staff and comfort of her old age certainly vanished on nearer view ; yet she liberally paid masters to attend me when I expressed a desire to continue my studies, and authorized me to open a subscription with the circulating library, as soon as I had hinted a wish for a higher sort of literature than that which was to be found in her cookery books. She even allowed me to read her to sleep of an evening with some romantic tale, provided it were not of a painful nature, and that all ended comfortably, for, as she wisely observed, "life, whether in fiction or reality, should always be like a good dinner, and close with the dessert."

We were enjoying ourselves after this fashion on a quiet winter's evening, and my god-mother had just dropped off into her usual doze, when

I heard a carriage stopping at the door. The bell was rung violently; Marianne opened, and in a few seconds entered the parlour.

" Madame," said she, with a bewildered look, " a lady—your sister, she says — wishes to see you."

I had never heard of my god-mother having more than one sister, who had died, or was said to have died, in America. I conjectured this was she or her ghost, and the horror-struck look of Mademoiselle Tournelle showed me she had come to the same conclusion. Before she could recover or even answer, the visitor entered. She was a tall, thin, pale-faced woman, clad in black from head to foot, with feathers in her bonnet, that waved like the plumes of a hearse, and a long black velvet cloak, not unlike a pall. Her slow, majestic pace completed her funereal appearance. She paused on the threshold, and exclaiming with a broken sob, " Where is she ? where is my own darling sister ? "

She opened her arms to receive my transported god-mother. But, apart the effort it would have been to rise so soon after dinner, Mademoiselle Tournelle was too much stupified

to dream of doing aught save staring with a
secret horror at her sister, who accordingly fell
upon her bosom, and vowed with many a sob,
" that since they had met again, death alone
should part them; that she—my god-mother
—need not fear, for that her own Rosalie would
never, never leave her."

I never saw so tearful and melancholy a
being as this same Rosalie. She embraced
her sister and wept ; she drew away to look
at her and wept, and when I thought she
had fairly given it up, she hugged her
again with another sob and a fresh burst
of tears. My god-mother endured all with
as much mental as physical helplessness :
to protest or resist was as impracticable a
feat as to leave her arm-chair and fly.

The mournful Rosalie, though still weeping abundantly, had enough self-possession
left to go and dismiss the fiacre at the door,
and haggle about the fare with the driver.
When this important task—which ended in
the utter discomfiture of the cabman—was
over, she ordered Marianne to take in her
luggage, and walked up-stairs herself, for
the purpose of selecting the best of her
sister's spare bed-rooms. My poor god-

mother never moved once all the time.
Alarmed at her mute despair, I sought to
comfort her, but all she could or would
say was that, " since Rosalie, instead of
being dead—as she ought to have been—
was alive and well, it must be she who
was destined to leave this world." She
closed her eyes and feebly shook her head
when I endeavoured to remove this painful impression. I perceived at supper how
deeply this idea had taken hold of her
mind. We had a hot fricassée of rabbit,
but scarcely had my god-mother tasted
the first mouthful, when she laid down
her fork, and giving me a mournful look,
exclaimed :

" No mushroom ! "

In her agitation, Marianne had—for the
first time—forgotten that important ingre-
dient, and my god-mother took this as a
clear warning that she was soon to be
called away from the good things of this
world. From that fatal day her appetite
declined visibly. The ghostlike Rosalie—
the mystery of whose reäppearance was
never cleared up — carried her off in six
weeks. I should have thought half the

time quite sufficient, but my god-mother had a strong constitution. For six weeks her breakfast was disturbed by the lamentations of Rosalie, who mourned to think that her darling sister's years would not permit them to be long together; at dinner she heard herself besought in pathetic accents " to be frugal—to remember that their dear father had died of apoplexy, and that their dearest mother was so dropsical!" When supper time came round, Rosalie wept over her and told her " she was fast breaking up." At the end of the six weeks my poor god-mother, fairly conquered, took to her bed and died.

I had not loved her very much, yet I grieved for her death. She had been kind in her way; besides, it is one of my weaknesses to get easily attached to the human faces around me. I moreover pitied my poor god-mother, and lamented her unhappy end. By her will, Mademoiselle Tournelle left her property to Marianne, " as a token of esteem for her high talents, and gratitude for her faithful services." A codicil gave me a dowry of ten thousand francs, of which the interest alone was at my disposal until I became of age. A second codicil bestowed "on the sister who had shortened her days—her forgiveness."

Rosalie was loud in her lament: "she had sacrificed herself to an ingrate, incapable of appreciating her devotion." Then suddenly her wrath vented itself upon me, whom she called "a little intrigante," and on Marianne, whom she accused of having poisoned her poor dear sister with her abominable cookery in general, and a perfidious dish of mushrooms in particular. How Marianne rose in her wrath, and turned Rosalie out of doors, is a matter foreign to the history of my experiences.

CHAPTER III.

BEHOLD me, kind reader, in a diligence once more, but this time on my road to Paris. I am nearly eighteen; my dowry yields me the magnificent income of three hundred francs, but I shrewdly conclude that this is not quite enough to live upon, and therefore proceed to the capital, where a host of pupils are, of course, ready to avail themselves of my talents,—I have taken pains, and am really an accomplished young lady. I go to Paris for three reasons: the first, that which I have mentioned; the second, that I am determined to see the world; the third, that Paris is the present residence of my step-mother, under whose guardianship I in some sort consider myself, and with whom I have kept up a distant correspondence. She coldly approves my resolve of remaining in some respectable boarding-school until I can procure pupils, or a situation as governess; and informs me that Joséphine and Louise have married advantageously in Normandy, our native province; but why she herself stays in Paris she does not mention. She offers me no home with her, nor, to say the truth, do I desire one, for my heart is still sore with the memory of old times.

My journey was uninteresting. Paris confused more than it dazzled me. The office of the diligence was not far from my step-mother's residence; I hired a fiacre, and was at her door within half an hour of my arrival. The house was mean, though clean; she lived on the fourth-floor in a small apartment, scantily furnished. This was strange for one of her elegant tastes and habits. She received me kindly, but coldly, as usual. We spoke of my god-mother.

"I wonder she did not leave you more than ten thousand francs," said Madame Delmare; "I thought she would adopt you."

"She was very kind," I replied; "I had no claim upon her, I have no claim on any one." My step-mother pressed her hand to her forehead; I thought she looked troubled. I hastened to speak of Joséphine and Louise.

"They are so happy," said the fond mother, with a sudden smile and a brightening look.

I understood all at once: she had given everything up to marry her plain daughters, and this thought could make the miserable little apartment a sunny and joyful place for her. But why was she not with either of them? why was she alone? I could not help putting the thought into words. She hastily replied "that it was her own choice, quite her own choice; she had always liked Paris." And she gave me an anxious look, as if she feared I might not believe her.

Why is it that, when I beheld her there alone and forsaken, hiding her poverty in the bosom of a great and strange city, the memory of every past kindness rose so strong within me, that my whole heart yearned towards her? and I could not but speak:

"Maman," said I, for I had always named her thus, "it so happens that we are both alone in this strange place. Is there anything to prevent us from being together? I will be no burden to you. Indeed, I fancy we might be happier together."

At first she did not answer.

"My poor child," she said at length, "my health is not very good : you would have but a dull life with me."

"I should like it, I should like it dearly," I eagerly exclaimed. "Pray let it be so. You will love me a little for my father's sake, and I will love you a great deal, not for his sake only, but for your own sake, and for all the good you did to one who had none on earth save you."

I laid my hand upon her arm and looked up into her face, for indeed my heart was in what I said, and I felt very much moved.

"Sylvie," answered my step-mother, in a tremulous tone, "you are a good child, with a kind heart. God will bless you for all this." And drawing me towards her, she kissed me and wept.

The joy her consent gave me showed me how much I loved her in my heart. I never spent a happier day or more pleasant evening. The reserve she had always inspired me with vanished at once. I talked incessantly; firstly, because joy has the effect of making me

voluble; and secondly, because it was so pleasant to hear my own voice calling her "maman."

"Maman, I shall have so many pupils,"
said I, arranging my books in the little drawing-
room. "Maman, I shall earn so much
money," I observed at dinner—it was rather a
frugal one. "I only fear, maman," said I in
the evening, "that I shall scarcely have any
time to be at home with you."

Maman smiled. She was sitting by the fire-
side, with something of mingled joy and sadness
in her look as it rested upon me. I sat on a
low stool at her feet, building my glorious
castles in the air, with the zeal and faith of an
architect of eighteen. They stood so clearly
before me. That very day, within two hours
of my arrival, I had taken my advertisement to
be inserted in the Petites Affiches : " A young
lady—well educated—good musician—English
and Italian—terms moderate ! " What parent
or guardian could resist this appeal, and be so
blind to the great rule of self-interest as not
to secure my services at once?

"Maman," I continued, in my random talk,
" you should always wear black silk, nothing
becomes you so well. Why have you no

flowers now? I know you are fond of them.
Shall we not remove from here? As I was
coming home from the newspaper office I saw
a charming fourth-floor to let, with a large
balcony, quite the thing for your flowers, and a
handsome room that would do so well for me
to have classes at home; for you see it would
be a great deal more pleasant for the pupils to
come to me—than for me to be running after
them, in wind, rain, and every weather; besides
the expense of taking omnibuses in order to be
in time."

"My dear child," said maman, a little
gravely, "you have not got the pupils yet."

"But they are coming," I confidently replied.

We took the apartment. I spent no little
of my ready money on furniture for the drawing-room, and especially on a large mahogany
table, covered with green baize, which I
destined for the "classes;" it was somewhat
dear, but one pupil at ten francs a month
would — as I proved to maman — cover the
expense in eight months and a half. Upon
the whole, I thought it cheap, and rejoiced over
my bargain.

There was only one circumstance which

mortified me: "the out-door pupils, whom it was so fatiguing to run after in wind, rain, and every weather," delayed making their appearance. I could not understand this. Had my advertisement appeared? It had. Were, then, the parents and guardians of Paris struck with moral blindness, that they so recklessly disregarded the advantages offered to them? I recapitulated inwardly. A young lady—well educated—good musician—English and Italian —terms moderate: And yet a whole fortnight had elapsed, and no answer had come.

"There is only one explanation possible," said I to maman; "some unprincipled governess has, by means as yet inexplicable to me—but I shall find it out—intercepted the answers of my unknown correspondents at the newspaper office—I shall have them sent here another time—and carried off my unhappy and deluded pupils. Nice teaching they will get from *her!* This is very tiresome, for I shall have to insert another advertisement. But after all," I consolingly added, "it is only a fortnight lost, for it stands to reason that I could not have accepted all the pupils."

Maman received this explanation with a

doubtful look, but she was unwilling to discourage me.

A second advertisement was, therefore, sent, with the wise precautions I have mentioned. But when two days had elapsed, and I received no reply, I could not help observing with some anxiety:

"I fear, maman, she has carried them all off. Of course they were all attracted by the first advertisement. Do you think it will be very long before I can find another supply?"

Maman's reply was more encouraging than definite; but I comforted myself with the "classes." I gloried, I may say I revelled, in the "classes." I beheld—in my mind's eye —the long table covered with inkstands, books, and papers, and surrounded by attentive pupils, who hung upon my words. I—preserving that gravity which should never desert a teacher—seriously expound that which it is my object to teach, patiently listen to timid objections, and gently explain all difficulties away. At the end of every month I receive the moderate sum of ten francs from each pupil—it is fifteen if they remain an hour extra, see last paragraph but one of the prospectus. These ten francs all put together

make a handsome pile of five-franc pieces,
which I display to the astonished gaze of
maman, and out of which I secretly buy her
a rich black silk dress. Instead, however, of
reproving me for my extravagance, she merely
says :

"Sylvie, my dear, your pupils are not
coming."

The dream vanishes at once, and I waken
with a perturbed spirit, for if I get no pupils,
what becomes of the "classes?" Fate, who
then entered the apartment under the shape
of our portress with a letter in her hand, spared
me the trouble of a reply. I broke the seal
with trembling fingers.

"A pupil! a dozen, for all I know," I
joyously exclaimed; "Mademoiselle Benoît—
an old aunt I will warrant, with a legion of
nieces—wants me; she lives close by; how
delightful!"

It was not in maman's power to moderate my transports, and so with a smile
and a sigh, and a recommendation to
secure advantageous terms, which I answered with a shrewd look, she saw me depart on my blissful errand.

I was at the door of Mademoiselle

Benoît in five minutes, but I walked up-
stairs with a cool business-like air, lest the
portress should by any means know my
errand, and suspect this was my first pupil.
Indeed, I was resolved to be greatly on
my guard, and I decided inwardly that
Mademoiselle Benoît must be very deep
to over-reach me. I found her in furnished
apartments on the second-floor, in her
boudoir; her favourite room, she said; I
cannot assert it was her only one, but it
was the first I entered, and the only door
I saw looked as if leading to a dark closet,
by which I do not mean to imply that a
whole suite of apartments did not extend
beyond.

Mademoiselle Benoît was about forty,
sallow and plain, but so juvenile in her
attire, that I looked quite matronly by her
side in my dress of sober brown. Half
rising from the sofa on which she was re-
clining, she languidly inquired my errand.
I explained. She looked incredulous. "Impossible!" she exclaimed. I nervously produced the letter. She eyed it like a person waking from a dream.

"Ah! I remember now," she thoughtfully

exclaimed ; " I had forgotten all about it. You need not be astonished, it is just like me."

I supposed she had a bad memory : but she shook her head. "Memory—no, it was not that ; but we would not speak on this subject. She had seen my advertisement, and wished to know whether I would mind devoting a few hours to her daily, as secretary, reader, and companion." This was not what I had hoped for, but I was in no mood to refuse. The next thing I supposed would be the discussion about terms, and here I was ready for Mademoiselle Benoît ; but without alluding to this subject she merely said :

"My nerves render this plan imperative. I must place myself and my too ardent feelings under the control of a calmer mind. Certain agitating books must be read slowly; certain deep emotions must be vented slowly. You understand."

I tried to look as if I did, but I was thinking of the terms. "Besides," she continued modestly, "unmarried—alone—without a male protector in this great city, where I am detained by a vexatious law-

suit—obliged to receive the visits of men
of business, I really cannot dispense with
the presence of a person of my own sex,
to whom I shall look for advice and protection." I felt confounded at the idea of
having to advise and protect a lady who
might, without any stretch of fancy, have
been my mamma. Heedless of this, she
proposed that I should begin my office
by reading Victor Hugo's last volume, and
she had already assumed a listening attitude,
when I faltered out something about
terms. She looked infinitely shocked.

"'Terms! money, mon Dieu! how could
some people be so very worldly? She
never thought of money."

I inwardly despised myself as a worshipper of mammon—well I might in the presence of such high-mindedness. She pursued: "Since the odious subject has been
mentioned, pray what are your terms? But
mind, I know as much of such things as a
baby."

Beautiful ignorance and charming confidence. With what agonizing nicety did I
calculate the exact sum I might conscien-
tiously ask. At length it came out: for

three hours a day, fifty francs a month.
" Fifty," she carelessly repeated, her mind
on other things, her eyes on the ceiling ;
then suddenly turning them upon me, she
added : " Don't you think you could come
for forty ? "

" I do not think I could," I replied, with
some emotion.

" But any one would, I assure you," was
her significant rejoinder.

This settled the matter. I perceived that
in my ignorance I had asked a salary so
high as to startle even this ingenuous lady.
I was distressed, I apologized ; I would
have come for thirty francs if she had
asked me.

" No apologies," she said, with a sigh ; "
" I admire, I envy your worldly wisdom.
Would I might acquire some of it. Vain
hope ! I, too heedless, too confiding, shall be
imposed upon to the end. You, so acute,
so penetrating—ah ! I envy you. And now
a few pages of Victor Hugo, if you please."

She once more assumed the listening
attitude. When we had done with Victor
Hugo we took up Lamartine : in short, we
went the round of French poets in two

hours. I occasionally besought Mademoiselle Benoît to explain various obscure and mysterious passages, with which she seemed particularly enraptured, but she only turned up her eyes, shook her head, and sighed. " I was happy not to understand such things; I should never seek to understand them; it was best to remain as I was. And now," she added, " will you be so good as to take a pen, a sheet of paper, and prepare to write? "

I complied, and listened with some curiosity, for I felt confident she was a muse, at the very least; but she only dictated the following letter:

" MY DEAR CICERO,

" Be not surprised at the strange handwriting. I have secured — a step you will approve—a companion, whose prudence and worldly wisdom will greatly benefit your poor heedless friend.

" I feel anxious about your health, not having seen you these two days. I need scarcely say that for the paltry law-suit I do not care. You know my foolish disinterestedness. My opponent, poor man, has set his heart on gaining his cause. Pray let him: I have a 'wealth in my thoughts, in my feelings, in my heart, he cannot touch. I would say come and dine with me to-morrow, did I not know your strict business habits ; but you will perhaps call in the afternoon to let me know how the case is going on. In the artistic point of view I feel deeply interested in it."

Mademoiselle Benoît, having signed this letter, requested me to fold it up, but suddenly recollecting herself, she begged of me to open it again: "there was a little post-scription to add."

I complied, and added the following P.S.

" By the merest chance — a letter from the country — I learned this morning that the grandfather of my opponent was a notorious gambler; that his eldest son, the father of my opponent, failed ; that his second son, the uncle of my opponent, was drowned in a very inexplicable sort of way; and that the first wife of my opponent died suddenly, she being then *alone* in the house with her husband.

" P.P. S.S. I mention these circumstances, thinking they may interest you."

The letter, now fairly finished, was di-

rected to a Monsieur Everard, whom I conjectured to be her lawyer, and Mademoiselle Benoît asked me to post it as I
was going home. I found maman uneasy
at my long absence. Sitting down at her
feet by the fire-side, I gave her a minute
account of all that had passed. When I
told her about the agreement she shook
her head. But when I concluded, and
looked up into her face somewhat anxiously, she only smiled kindly, and said,
as she smoothed my hair, " I was a good
child, and with a little more knowledge
of the world I would do very well."

I felt relieved, for, to say the truth,
reader, I had begun to fear that Mademoiselle Benoît had over-reached me, and
that I had not been quite successful with
my first pupil.

Nothing worth mentioning occurred for
three weeks, during which I found no other
scholar. I comforted myself by thinking of
the " classes." I had ceased to mention them,
having a vague notion that maman, though
unwilling to discourage me, was getting
sceptical on this subject, and even looked
on the green table with an eye of disfavour.

I wrote—for Mademoiselle Benoît—almost daily epistles to Monsieur Everard, whom I never saw, but to whom—and this was really provoking—I had to describe myself as "the grave adviser and prudent worldly friend" of my employer. She informed me at the end of the three weeks that her law-suit was over; a great point, and that she had won; a secondary point, of course. Monsieur Everard was to dine with her the next day; but unless I consented to be present, she could not think of dining alone even with a single man of his years and gravity. I yielded, and accordingly dressed a little, a very little, better than usual for the occasion. Monsieur Everard was already there when I arrived. He was a tall, stiff man, but he did not look more than thirty, though grave enough for double that age. He wore a pair of green spectacles, which gave him a sort of impenetrable look, and which I considered symbolical of the mysteries of the law. I thought he eyed me with some surprise; he had probably expected to find his client's "grave adviser" somewhat older. He soon resumed his conversation with our hostess: they were talking about the law-

suit. She had already—charming oblivious-
ness—forgotten all about the damages.

"It was very foolish; she knew it was;
but now, positively, how much was it?"

"Fifteen thousand francs," shortly answered
the lawyer.

"Oh! of course: how could I? And the
costs you say—"

"Fall on your antagonist, who being nearly
ruined—"

"Poor man," quickly interrupted Mademoiselle Benoît.

"Asks for time to settle his account."

"Impossible," she said, with a deep sigh;
"I have—you know my weakness—given my
brother my solemn word of honour there shall
be no delay; but pray let him know I pity
him; pray do."

"I believe he has not the money," continued Monsieur Everard.

"How unprincipled!" cried Mademoiselle
Benoît, colouring, "but I remember he has
land."

"Do you wish for a saisie?" coolly asked
the lawyer.

"Oh! you cruel man, to hint at such a
thing!"

" Then you object to a saisie ? "

" Alas ! why is it inevitable ? "

" Mademoiselle Benoît, I am a plain man :
do you or do you not wish for a saisie ? "

She protested he was the most pitiless
man in existence : that he put things into
her head of which it grieved her to think;
that since no other means remained, she must
of course say "yes;" but that she begged
him not to harrow her foolish feelings any
longer with so distressing a subject. A
peculiar smile curled Monsieur Everard's
nether lip, but he made no reply, and bowed
coldly. Our charming hostess, anxious not to
leave us under a painful impression, soon
recovered her flow of spirits. She gaily taxed
the lawyer with his gravity, and protested
I was more sedate than ever.

" You have no idea," said she, addressing
him, " what a prudent, calculating head that
is. How I am checked, subdued, and
brought down to a sober mood, by this grave
worldly little friend of mine. Oh ! you can
have no idea."

" Indeed ! " said he, with the same smile.

I coloured, and felt heartily ashamed of my
worldliness. Dinner was not ready yet, and

Mademoiselle Benoît proposed a walk in the
Tuileries; we acceded. She retired to the room
that looked like a dark closet, and in a few
minutes appeared in an elaborate toilette, that
threw me quite in the shade.

The day was fine, the garden was thronged,
and our walk seemed very pleasant. We had
not proceeded far along the broad avenue
of horse chestnuts, when we met two ladies
and a gentleman. They gave us a peculiar
look, and the gentleman observed in a low
tone : "What a charming blonde." They
passed on, and left me in a flutter. The
green spectacles of Monsieur Everard, whose
arm I held, were on me in a second, then as
sharply turned towards Mademoiselle Benoît ;
her hair was dark. The compliment could
not be for her, yet I wondered, and felt
incredulous. Two ladies walking together
had already passed us ; they looked at my
companions first, then at me, lingered behind,
and one whispered to the other : "The blonde
is lovely." What woman can doubt her
beauty when it is praised by another woman ?
I confess I began to feel uncomfortable on
this subject. Had I been handsome all
along without knowing it ? Novel heroines

always were unconscious. Perhaps I was a heroine! I will not weary the reader by repeating all the exclamations of admiration which were bestowed on the lovely blonde during our hour's walk. I began to find that there was nothing so astonishing in all this; I had never been counted handsome in the province; but who did not know the discrimination of Parisian taste?

I was seated at dinner near Monsieur Everard, but neither the lawyer nor his green spectacles occupied me much : I was thinking of the discovery I had made.

"I congratulate you on your triumph, Mademoiselle," he observed, after the soup.

I blushed, and thought he might have spared my modesty.

"What triumph?" asked our hostess.

"I should have said the triumph of your taste. Did you not hear every one admiring the blonde on your bonnet?"

"Oh! it was the blonde then," I cried, quite bewildered. The green spectacles were upon me directly. I became crimson. He said nothing, but smiled so significantly that I felt I hated him.

"Yes," sighed Mademoiselle Benoît, "I

have been very extravagant; my prudent friend there would never forgive me if she knew how much that blonde cost."

Monsieur Everard gave me another look, but he had mercy enough to remain silent.

I went home vexed with the keen-sighted lawyer, vexed with myself and my own foolish vanity. Had I not eyes to see the blonde on Mademoiselle Benoît's bonnet ?

I was so mortified that I did not notice maman's smiling and amused face ; but she noticed my downcast look and questioned me. I told her what had happened ; she laughed, and bade me not mind Monsieur Everard or Mademoiselle Benoît.

" You have found other friends," she said. "What do you think of Mademoiselle finding you a husband ? "

My breath seemed gone at this strange suggestion.

" Yes," pursued maman, " Mademoiselle declares that she has found you a husband."

I have not yet mentioned Mademoiselle. Her name was Leonie Moreau, I believe, but I am not sure. No one had ever dreamed of calling her otherwise than Mademoiselle. She was fifty, brown as a berry, stout, and

brisk as a bee, and she was Mademoiselle for
every one in the house in which she had lived
for the last thirty-three years. The door of
our apartment faced hers : we met her often
on the staircase, and saw a good deal of her on
her balcony, which was a continuation of ours.
Maman had a distant acquaintance with some
of Mademoiselle's relatives. Thus our knowledge of her began, and as Mademoiselle had
a warm heart and a lively tongue, our friendship progressed rapidly; to me she took an
especial fancy. She found me strikingly like
a young sister of hers, who had died some
thirty years before, and she liked me for the
resemblance more, I believe, than for my own
particular merits. She never saw me water-
ing flowers on the balcony without a tear in
her eye, that did not check the pleasant and
habitual smile on her lips, or the cheerful
" Good morning " with which she always
greeted me. In my " classes " and attempts to
procure pupils she entered warmly, and did
her best, I am sure, to second me, but uselessly ;
and it probably was her failure in that quarter
that had suggested to her the propriety of
finding me a husband. How she meant to
set about this strange task, and what sort of

husband it was to be, maman could not or
would not tell me.

"Go on the balcony and water your flowers,"
she said, "Mademoiselle will be there, and she
will tell you all about it."

At first I said I would not go; then curiosity proved stronger than pride: I filled my
watering-pot and I stepped out. A brown
face immediately appeared between two tall
laurel trees standing in pots, and a beaming
smile welcomed me.

"What a lovely evening, Mademoiselle
Sylvie," said the gay voice of Mademoiselle.

A rosy flush spread above the opposite roof,
and faded away into the heavenly blue at the
zenith. It was a fine evening, and I said so
whilst I watered a rose tree. Mademoiselle's
head stretched out as far as it could go, and
she confidentially whispered:

"I wish you would draw a little nearer, my
dear."

I obeyed in some confusion, and she half
said, half whispered:

"I cannot speak loud on account of that
odious little thing down-stairs. I am confident
she listens; else how could things that I have
not mentioned to more than half a dozen

trustworthy people get wind? It looks suspicious."

I confessed it did.

" Well, then, my dear, let us speak low. I
mentioned to your mamma this afternoon a
little scheme of my own. I want you to
marry a young cousin of mine. Of course
you must know more about it before you
reply. Well, then, here is an exact and most
accurate description of my cousin. He is
twenty-eight, tall, dark-haired, and blue-eyed :
so he will just suit you, who are rather short
and fair. He has handsome features, and a
most pleasant countenance. So much for his
person : his temper is angelic, sweet, and most
amiable. His means are not great as yet ;
but he makes money enough, and requires but
a small dot. Your ten thousand francs will
do. He is to spend the evening with me
after to-morrow, and you will just drop in by
chance. He will know you by your dress,
which I shall describe—not a word !—*he* will
not know that *you* know anything about it :
so please to look as cool and as careless as
possible. I mention the circumstance of the
dress because some other girl might call, and
though he knows almost all the young ladies

with whom I am acquainted, yet there might
be a stray one, and a mistake might occur.
What will you wear; white muslin or blue?
you look well in both."

I had a vision of a fastidious young Sultan,
handsome and scornful, sitting on Mademoiselle's drawing-room sofa, and thence surveying,
through his critical eye-glass, a series of fair or
dark girls passing before him with their most
fascinating looks, and I firmly resolved that one
of these I should not be. But Mademoiselle
was a wilful little woman. I therefore merely
said that I was very much obliged to her, and
that I should think over her kind proposal. She
looked at me doubtfully.

" You are not committed in the least," she
said; " I have told him nothing, save that you
are a good daughter, a charming girl, and that
you have ten thousand francs. He does not
even know your name, nor where you live, nor
the colour of your hair. So you see, Mignonne,
I could not do things more delicately."

I repeated that I was very much obliged to
her, and succeeded in changing the subject of
discourse. When I went in, I told maman all
that had passed, and protested I would not go
and be looked at.

" You are wrong, my dear," said my step-
mother, " Mademoiselle's cousin is an employé ;
I believe, in a worldly point of view, it would
be a good match. Besides, what do you risk
or lose by going ? Mademoiselle has managed
everything so well that you are not in the least
committed. You will be looked at by a man
who does not even know your name. Where
is the harm ? Besides, is it not so that
marriages are managed ? You must not be
romantic, my love."

In short, I was talked and reasoned into com-
pliance.

But when the evening came my heart again
failed me, and I begged of maman not to insist
on my meeting that Monsieur Renaud, such I
understood to be his name, as I really did not
feel equal to the effort. She shook her head,
and said that youth would be romantic, but
she did not insist, and accordingly sent in a
few words of apology to Mademoiselle.

CHAPTER IV.

I FELT rather amused at the idea of Monsieur Renaud's disappointment, and a little curious to know how he had spent his evening. Accordingly, I went out on the balcony early the next morning, and had scarcely stepped out when Mademoiselle's window flew open, and Mademoiselle herself, heedless of curl papers and night-cap, appeared with as much wrath on her brown face as could ever find room there.

"Oh! you naughty thing," she said, "if you only knew the mischief you have done! But I must be fair; you never could imagine it; no one could: it is that odious little thing down-stairs! Monsieur Renaud came as agreed. I recapitulated all your good qualities. I *will* say it to vex you. I told him you were discreet, prudent, without a particle of vanity, and that you were to wear a blue dress. Well, he sat waiting, burning with impatience, for he is a very ardent young man,

when who should walk in but Eugénie and
her mother, and what should Eugénie wear
but a blue dress! I made signs to him that
she was not the right one, and concluded all
was right; but, my dear, I was so provoked.
It must have been the horrid little thing
down-stairs that let that bold little flirt and
her designing mother know there was a future
husband then with me! How they behaved
I will not tell you: it was disgraceful!
Eugénie made love to my cousin before my
very eyes! If you had only come in; well—
well—I have not had many such evenings. At
length they left, and before I could open my
lips, out flew my cousin: 'What a charming,
artless girl! I declare I am quite smitten!'
'It was not the right one!' I screamed.
'This is a bold, forward little flirt. I tell
you it was not the right one. *She* could not,
or rather would not, come.' 'Well, then, let
her stay,' he replies, 'I am quite satisfied with
the one I have seen.' I declare I cried with
vexation; but he only laughed, and if he
marries that little coquette, I shall lay it all to
you."

I was half amused and half annoyed at
this account. I did not care about Monsieur

Renaud; but I had wanted him to be disappointed, to be shown that girls were not at his bidding; not to be courted by a Mademoiselle Eugénie, and to fall in love with her forthwith. However, what was done was done, and I had no right to complain if another had prevailed where I had not attempted to succeed. I was sorry to perceive, however, that maman was quite vexed. "You will never get on in the world, my dear," she said, a little sharply, and then she chid herself for this little burst of temper, and kissing me, said I was a good child for all that.

My lesson that day proved particularly disagreeable. Mademoiselle Benoît could not hold her peace on my worldly-mindedness and my prudence; and Monsieur Everard, who was present, could not help dropping hints that provoked me beyond all patience. It appeared from his speech that artless, unassuming modesty was the charm of woman in his eyes. With a sigh Mademoiselle Benoît asked what woman was without that? And so they went on echoing each other, until I had a great mind to get up and walk out. I did not, for several very excellent reasons; but I came home in no very pleasant mood. I went out on the balcony,

certainly in no hopes of meeting Mademoiselle, but there she was however, bright and
beaming as usual.

"My dear," she said, "I have such news
for you. You know what I told you about
my cousin, and how smitten he was with
Mademoiselle Eugénie's artlessness—"

"Indeed, Mademoiselle," I interrupted,
feeling vexed at hearing so much on that subject in one day, "indeed I do not care about
Monsieur Renaud or Mademoiselle. I am
delighted they are mutually pleased; but I
really wish to hear no more about them."

Mademoiselle looked at me with some surprise.

"My dear," she said, "how warmly you
speak. I meant no harm, and, moreover, it is
all right. My cousin called this morning to
beg to see the right one, and to assure me
that when he professed himself so pleased
with Mademoiselle Eugénie, he was only jok-
ing—he has a vast deal of humour. In short,
he is to come and dine with me this evening,
and you must come too."

Maman supported this suggestion so
strongly, that I was obliged to yield. It was
nearly dinner time, and I had barely half an

hour for my toilette. I said anything would
do, but maman, who was unusually fastidious,
seemed to think that nothing could do. At
length we were both ready, and with some
trepidation on my part, we crossed the landing,
and rang at Mademoiselle's door. Mademoiselle's blooming Norman servant-girl opened
to us with a smile, and ushered us in. Mademoiselle herself, in the splendour of a pink
cap and a brown silk dress, rushed forward to
meet us, and clasped us both in her arms.
She seemed very much excited, and almost
beside herself.

"My dears," she exclaimed, in an under
tone, "I am so glad. My cousin is burning
with impatience. He is a very ardent young
man. I am sure he is quite in a fever of ex-
pectation. I know I was. Pray walk in to
the drawing-room."

If I had not felt pretty certain that the
fever was all of Mademoiselle's feeling or
imagination, this speech of hers would have
made me very uncomfortable, but the ardour
of a man who searched for a wife in the metho-
dical fashion adopted by Mademoiselle's cousin
seemed to me very doubtful, so doubtful indeed, that there was scarce a flush in my

cheek when I followed maman into the drawing-room. A gentleman, who sat looking over
a book of engravings, rose as we entered.
He looked at me, and I looked at him. I saw
Monsieur Everard.

"My cousin, Monsieur Everard Renaud,"
said Mademoiselle; "Madame Delmare, her
daughter, Mademoiselle Sylvie Delmare."

I certainly do not know what sort of a feeling sinking in the ground produces in the
person so sunk, but it seemed to me then that
to sink through the polished oak floor on
which I stood, and vanish no matter where,
would have been pleasanter than to face Monsieur Everard. True, he behaved decorously
and well; looked grave and unconscious, but
could I forget what we had met for, and could
he? Impossible, we both knew it: it was
dreadful. But from the very misery of the
position came a sort of relief. I felt convinced
that the quiet, prudent Monsieur Everard, so
strangely described as an ardent and enthusi-
astic young man, would never bestow a second
thought on the girl of whose credulity and
vanity he had obtained such recent proofs.
This quite set me at my ease. Monsieur
Everard was no one, and I spoke and acted

under this feeling. The dinner went off very well; the evening was pleasant. M. Everard made himself agreeable, Mademoiselle was in ecstasies, and maman very well pleased.

"My dear," said she, when we retired, "I like that Monsieur Renaud. He is sensible: he is a man of the world, and if you could marry him, or one like him, I should be well pleased."

I laughed. "Dear maman," I said, "Monsieur Renaud and Monsieur Everard are one. So just fancy what a chance I have of either."

Maman was at first taken aback, then she said she did not see that. I interrupted her to declare with some warmth, that though I was sure Monsieur Everard would not have me, yet even if he would, nothing should make me have so hard and disagreeable a man. Maman sighed, and feared I was romantic, but did not insist.

The next day I went to my lesson as usual; Mademoiselle Benoît was with her lawyer, and the said lawyer chose to be very impertinent, as I thought. He said nothing that I could quarrel with, but his looks and smiles, when Mademoiselle Benoît descanted, as usual, on my

merits and the advantage I was to her were
more than I could endure. I felt injured, and
went home in such bad humour that it was
some time before I perceived maman's pale
face, that still bore the trace of recent tears.
At length I was struck with both, and going up hastily to her, I asked what had
happened.

"A great misfortune, my dear child," she
replied, in a tremulous tone.

"What is it, maman?"

"The agent de change, to whom I had confided my rentes to dispose of, has absconded to
Belgium."

This was indeed a woeful blow, but I comforted maman as well as I could. I besought
her not to leave me for either of her daughters,
who did not want her as I did; then I said it
would only be removing to a cheaper apartment and living a little more frugally; that I
would get scholars yet, and "classes" too, and
that all would be comfortable. She refused for
a long time, saying she had no claim upon
me—which I warmly denied—but she ended
by yielding. Dear maman! her heart was sore
indeed, but she did not wish me to think her
own children would be loath to receive her, and

I felt as anxious not to let her see I knew the bitter truth.

"And now, maman," said I, "just let me write down the name of that agent de change. Who knows but Monsieur Everard may give us some good advice!"

She sighed and shook her head as she uttered the name: "Monsieur Durand of Hâvre."

The pen dropped from my fingers. Oh! it was too much, too much indeed. I felt it, and fairly burst into tears.

"Sylvie! my dear child! what is the matter?" cried maman.

"Alas!" I exclaimed, weeping still, "it is that same Monsieur Durand who has got my money."

We passed a weary evening, endeavouring to comfort each other, but feeling sad indeed. Maman was more distressed for me than for herself. Every time her eyes fell upon me they filled with tears. I knew why. The home which would receive her would be closed upon me. She felt it keenly.

"Oh!" she exclaimed, in a tone of deep sorrow, "what would your poor father say?"

"That you acted for the best," I replied, kissing her.

CHAPTER V.

I FEAR my eyes were still red when I called the following day on Mademoiselle Benoît. She was engaged in the uncongenial task of receiving a large sum of money, which her lawyer methodically counted over to her. He bowed and smiled—much I cared about his smiling!—but she never raised her eyes from the table: it was full five minutes before they had done.

" There, take it away," she then contemptuously exclaimed, addressing some imaginary worshipper of mammon. But no one appearing, she rose with a sigh and removed the treasure to the neighbouring room, whence we heard various sounds of unlocking and locking up again. I thought to take this moment to address Monsieur Everard, whom, for many reasons, I wished to acquaint with what had happened; but he seemed so entirely absorbed by his law papers, and as he turned them over his countenance looked so severe, that my heart failed me.

" Mademoiselle," said he, suddenly glancing up and catching my look before I had time to withdraw it, " do you feel unwell ? "

I told him my little story in a low tone. He looked concerned, and took both the name of the agent de change and our address ; " it was very unfortunate indeed ; " and his accent was more kind and compassionate than I could have expected from him. Mademoiselle Benoît, who had done locking up, had no such weakness.

" What !" she exclaimed, with a noble disdain of riches, " the loss of the vile metal called gold can affect you thus ? Oh ! the worldliness of this world !"

She continued to comfort me by dwelling so forcibly on the charms of poverty and the miseries of the rich, that I would have concluded the agent de change was a humane and benevolent philanthropist, bent on relieving me and my fellow-victims from the intolerable burden of money, if the worldliness which was so strong within me had not absolutely revolted against any such conclusion.

As I was leaving her, Mademoiselle Benoît handed me the sum of forty francs. Our " lessons," as she was pleased to term them,

were over with the law-suit, and she was returning to her native province. She warmly
thanked me for the excellent advice I had
given her, and the judicious control I had
exercised over her feelings. "But, my dear
friend," said she, as we parted, "pray do not
be so worldly; it dries up the heart."

Thus ended my brief connexion with my
first pupil. I advertised again, but, alas! in
vain.

Though I drew up a prospectus of my in-
tended "classes," I grieve to say that the
public were so injudicious as not to be
captivated with my scheme. The classes, in
short, proved a failure, and the green table
which filled all our drawing-room being pronounced a perfect bore, was on the point of
being sold to a broker, when Monsieur Everard,
learning our intention, purchased it. This
leads me to observe that the lawyer called upon
us almost every day, to tell us that the run-
away agent de change had been heard of, or
would be heard of soon, or had not been heard
of at all. This did not mend the matter much,
but maman was greatly touched with his disinterested zeal, and declared to me she had
never met so kind and obliging a man. It

vexed her to perceive that he did not stand very high in my favour; but, to be candid, the little he did say to me was always of an annoying and provoking nature; for after appealing, on one point or another, to my prudence and worldly wisdom, with so much gravity that I could not but think him in earnest, and candidly gave him my opinion, he would suddenly turn round, and looking at me from under his green spectacles, say with his own peculiar smile:

"And so, Mademoiselle Sylvie, you thought you were the blonde"—he did not add the epithet "lovely," but I knew he thought it— "ah! well, to see how the wisest of us can be deceived!"

The reader must not imagine that, because pupils did not come and "classes" would not answer, I remained idle. No; we had been so fortunate as to procure some embroidery from a large shop, and we worked from morning till night to eke out a scanty subsistence. I was grieved to see maman thus reduced; for my part, I was young, full of hope, and did not mind it. Never, indeed, had I been so happy. What were the comforts of my early home, when maman's heart was estranged from me? What was the good living of my poor god-mother's house compared to the pleasures of this humble home, where I loved and was loved? For maman loved me now: I saw it every day in her kindly look, and heard it in her gentle voice.

I had come home one evening with some work, when I found Monsieur Everard in earnest conversation with maman.

"Mademoiselle Sylvie," said he, "I have news for you."

"Indeed," I shortly replied, for he had teased me about the blonde that same morning.

"Yes, the agent de change was arrested this morning, having been fool enough to come back to Paris. I am happy to say Madame Delmare's rentes were all found upon him."

I clapped my hands and kissed maman. "There," I cried joyously, taking her work from her, "let me never see you at this again."

"Be quiet," said she, smiling, "you have not heard all Monsieur Everard has to say."

"Oh! I know," I shrewdly observed, "my ten thousand francs are found too."

"Wisely inferred," said he, with a smile, " but, alas, I grieve to say your ten thousand francs are gone, quite gone ; " and he spoke as if he felt glad of it.

I felt disappointed, but I soon rallied. " Well," said I, resolutely, " I can work ; cannot I, maman ? "

" Yes, my dear, but you have not yet heard Monsieur Everard."

I looked at him with some surprise. He did not speak, but fidgetted on his chair, coughed, rose, took a turn across the room, then came back, still silent, to his seat. I looked at maman : she was endeavouring to repress a smile.

" Mademoiselle," said he, whilst a faint tinge of colour rose to his cheek, " I was explaining to Madame Delmare, when you entered, a wish I have for some time entertained, and which has obtained her approbation. I am a man of few words ; forgive me if, without further preparation, I simply ask : Will you become my wife ? "

He looked at me ; I remained mute. I felt astonished, and not triumphant, reader, but very much touched. I was neither rich nor handsome ; Monsieur Everard was no

heedless romantic man : I felt it was not
common affection and esteem had urged
him to this offer.

" Sylvie," anxiously said maman, " why do
you not answer ? "

Monsieur Everard said nothing, but looked
at me with evident uneasiness. I had remained silent, not because I knew not what
I felt, but because I knew not how to say it ;
I did not say it even then, but simply held
out my hand to him. He took it, and with
more gallantry than I could have expected
from him, raised it to his lips. I turned
my head away that he might not see my
eyes filling with tears ; Maman was suddenly
seized with a cold in her head ; even Monsieur
Everard did not quite succeed in preserving a
business-like composure ; but we all three
felt happy, and soon recovered, each keeping
up the pretence of not feeling a bit concerned.

He remained to dinner. He looked a little
awkward : I believe that in his heart he
feared I would retaliate for the past ; but
my only attempt in this way was to ask
for the green spectacles to be removed. They
vanished at my bidding, and allowed me to

perceive that the eyes they shaded had nothing amiss; but the whole countenance looked strange without them; I felt it thus, and before ten minutes had elapsed I said:

"Pray put on your spectacles again."

He smiled and obeyed. Our courtship was brief; it was his wish; it was maman's wish; what could I do but yield up the point quietly?

I have now been married ten years. I will give the reader no account of my married experiences, but simply describe to him the picture I behold as I write. It is winter: my husband is sitting by the fire-side, talking to Joseph, our eldest child. In her easy chair, on the other side of the fire-place, sits my dear maman; ay, mine, though no drop of the same blood flows in our veins. A child is on her knee, a little brunette, whose dark hair she smooths from her forehead with a gentle touch and a wistful glance; but, reader, that child is not mine; it is all that remains of her poor daughter Louise, who died a year ago, the broken-hearted widow of a ruined man. Joséphine offered to bring up the orphan with her own children, but maman jealously refused. She went for her

little Louise, brought her home, never allows
a hand save her own or mine to touch her,
and is always tracing in her features a likeness
no one save herself can see ; for Louise, though
dark, is truly pretty.

My child is that little blonde who now en-
deavours to attract her grandmamma's attention ; and see how maman hastens to make
room for her by the side of Louise, and tries
to look as if one were not dearer than the
other. But children are restless : Joseph
leaves his father, and Louise immediately
jumps down to join him in a game. Hen-
riette, happy in the exclusive possession of her
grandmamma, remains nestling with her. But
though maman encircles her caressingly, her
thoughtful look still follows Louise. She
smiles at her joyous spirits, at the patronizing
tone of Joseph, at the affection of the two
children, and she makes for the future, plans
which I read with a smile. She is already
fidgetting herself to know whether Louise
will be rich enough for Joseph ; she is project-
ing impossible savings out of her narrow income, in order to treasure her up a dowry.
Dear maman, were it not premature to speak
of such a thing,—Joseph is eight and Louise

five,—I might tell you that the point is already settled between myself and my husband. Should they be willing, a little money shall neither prevent the happiness of two loving hearts nor the fulfilment of your cherished dream : that the child of your child may become more closely linked to her on whom you have so long bestowed the name, and who truly feels for you the love of a daughter.

THE END.

JOHN CHILDS AND SON, PRINTERS.

www.ingramcontent.com/pod-product-compliance
Lightning Source LLC
Chambersburg PA
CBHW020902020726
47497CB00005B/1513